Molly's Stallion

J.M. Shaw

Royal Fireworks Press
Unionville, New York

Library of Congress Cataloging-in-Publication Data

Shaw, J. M.
  Molly's stallion / J.M. Shaw.
      p. cm.
  Summary: After saving a foal born with a broken leg from
being euthanized, twelve-year-old Molly, who lives on her
family's struggling horse farm in Ocala, Florida, tries to
raise him to become a champion race horse.
  ISBN 978-0-88092-769-7 (pbk. : alk. paper)
  [1. Horses--Fiction. 2. Thoroughbred horse--Fiction. 3.
Horse racing--Fiction. 4. Ocala (Fla.)--Fiction.] I. Title.
  PZ7.S5369Mo 2010
  [Fic]--dc22

2010000909

Royal Fireworks Press
First Avenue, PO Box 399
Unionville, NY 10988-0399
(845) 726-4444
FAX: (845) 726-3824
email: mail@rfwp.com
website: rfwp.com

ISBN: 978-0-88092-769-7

Printed and bound in the United States of America using vegetable-based inks on acid-free, recycled paper and environmentally-friendly cover coatings by the Royal Fireworks Printing Co. of Unionville, New York.

CHAPTER ONE

A Stormy Birth

Florida lightning zippered across the sky illuminating the last few stalls of the Grimaldi's barn. Power was lost early in the storm, and an old gasoline powered generator provided fractured light to the house but not the barn. Eerie shafts of light rebounded throughout the barn, and Molly held a lantern as still as she could and stared wide-eyed as her father and the hired hand Manuel ripped old sheets in strips. Marty Grimaldi had a frustrated look on his face, and he held the mare's head down as she thrashed in a mountain of straw. Amazing Grace was a beautiful golden palomino, but right now her mouth was frothy and her skin shiny with slather, and she moaned and bucked, and Manuel tried to stand clear of legs that unexpectedly flashed out with astonishing power. The lantern swung in Molly's hands, and she could see the horse's eyes were huge and dilated. Molly had never been allowed to see a foal being born, and now her father wasn't sure he had made the right decision for her to see this one.

"Oh, Manny," her father said to the hand, "she's breeched. Any chance you can get the vet out of bed?"

"Not in this storm, boss," Manuel said. "By the time I can get there and back, you know it'll be too late."

"What's 'breeched,' Daddy?"

"Honey," her father answered, "Most of the time a foal will come straight out head and front legs first, but Manny and I think this one's turned a little and the foal's legs may be tucked under its body."

"That's bad?"

"I won't lie. It can be very bad. The longer it stays turned the more possible damage to Grace and her foal. There's not much we can do."

"So what will you do?"

"We'll wait. See, there's a birth canal—kind of like a tunnel—and that's the only way for the colt to come out safe and unharmed. We don't want the foal to come feet tucked back, so we'll wait and see if it turns the right way for us. The foal is ready to be born now, but we can wait a while."

"Yeah, but what if it doesn't turn, Daddy? What if it stays breeched?"

"Then there can be damage to the mother and the foal."

"Could they die?"

"Yes."

Molly became very quiet and tried to hold the lantern especially still. Manuel turned the mare with loving and practiced hands and hoped the movement might make the life inside turn in the right direction. Manuel was drenched in sweat and, every few moments he used all his strength to move Grace from one position to another. All the while Marty Grimaldi held a giant head in his hands and he whispered and petted Amazing Grace's matted mane. She struggled one moment and calmed the next, but it was more than clear that the next few hours would determine the fate of two lives. Eleven months of pregnancy had come down to these precious moments and there was nothing to be done.

"Dad," Molly said to her father, "I'm worried. What happens if the foal doesn't turn? Just tell me that and I won't ask any more questions."

"Molly, I don't lie to you. I didn't lie when I said your mother would likely die and I won't lie to you now. At first light I'm going to send you to get the vet and he will come and operate on Grace. You know the colt has to come out and I can't tell you how the operation will go. Grace could die and the colt too. Sometimes one lives and the other doesn't. There's no way of telling. Why don't you go up to the house and make some coffee for Manny and me? Any way this goes we'll be up all night. I'll need your help in the morning feeding the other horses so after making the coffee, you should go up to bed."

"Let me stay until the vet comes. I won't want to see anything as terrible as that, but I want to be here until then. I won't sleep with the storm and all this going on here."

"Fair enough. You go get coffee and some of those muffins from breakfast. I want you to boil some extra water and leave it hot on the stove. You grab that yellow slicker out from the tack room and cover your head. You hear?"

Molly did as told and ran toward the house with a tattered raincoat over her head. The rain was coming in slants now and every few seconds lightning ripped across the sky. The ruts in the road were brimming over with water and Molly was wet to the knees by the time she reached the porch. She looked toward the barn and could see flickering lantern light through the broken slats in the barn. Of the twenty horses still left on the Grimaldi farm, Amazing Grace had always been the most majestic and beautiful and now the palomino and her foal might die. None of the kids in the booming communities nearby understood life on a farm and there was no one she could share her feelings with but her father and Manny. On a farm, life and death are played out every day and the other kids would never understand the scene happening down at the barn. Molly was only twelve, but she had seen and done more than any half dozen of the kids that invaded the Ocala area now that farms were being subdivided and sold to developers.

Molly put on a huge pot of coffee to boil and fished thermos containers from under the sink that would help the coffee stay stinging hot throughout the night. Next she put a five-gallon pot on the back burner and used a container to fill it nearly to the top. She guessed her father would want hot water to keep Grace clean during the birth and extra water to clean the foal before it was wrapped in blankets to make it through the night. She went to her bedroom and shucked off wet jeans and found a fresh pair and, pulling her old boots over dry white socks, she felt dry and warm for the first time in several hours.

Molly was lean and tall, and her reddish blonde hair was braided and nearly down to her waist. While she was convinced she'd never be as pretty as her mother had been, Molly was naturally beautiful and her blonde hair was complimented by green eyes and light freckles along her nose and cheekbones. She looked in the full-length mirror in the hallway and decided, for a girl who had been up most of the night, she wasn't terrible looking. The water in the giant pot was beginning to gurgle, and Molly returned to the kitchen to pour coffee and get back out to the barn. Maybe Amazing Grace was doing better.

Molly filled the biggest thermos with black coffee and filled the smaller one with coffee mixed with cream and too much sugar that she would sip while the men drank bitter black liquid from tarnished cups in the tack room. She left the big pot of hot water on the stove and kept the burner on warm and she'd return for hot water at her father's direction. She shut off the lights to save the generator's life and fuel and, throwing the yellow slicker over her head, she went out on the porch carrying the containers of coffee and a Tupperware container of cookies and muffins her grandmother had dropped off in the morning. Daddy and Manny had to be hungry but a full meal would have to wait until tomorrow. She eased down the stairs and into the slop of the path to the barn and pelting rain. She held her arms outstretched for balance and to keep the rain from splashing up on fresh jeans. Again lightning ripped across the sky with silver veins that seemed to reach the ground a thousand or so feet away from the barn. Molly tried to hurry and momentarily hydroplaned across the mud until she regained her footing. Back in the barn, she went into the tack room and poured blazing hot coffee for the men.

"Manny," she asked the hired hand, "how's it going? Is the foal starting to turn the way you want?"

"I'm afraid not, baby girl," Manny said. "Grace is going to foal very soon. See how she's open down there? That means the foal is already in the canal and we'll see what we see. I dunno. Maybe everything will be okay. As soon as the phones come back on we'll call the vet and have him come right out. We won't need the operation, but that doesn't mean we're out of trouble. Your dad and I are both relatively sure the foal's in distress."

"Distress?"

"Manny's just trying to say that a birth like this one will come with problems," her father explained, "I don't remember a breech where something wasn't wrong. I never lie to you. We need the foal to come quickly now—the faster the less damage."

But the foal did not come quickly and Amazing Grace thrashed in the hay and blankets and Molly just stared. Across the way, in stall number six, Dashaway Dancer kicked at his stall door. A jet-black stallion with a white star in the middle of his forehead, Dashaway Dancer was father of the foal and now he craned his neck to see what was happening in the corner of the barn. He stomped and kicked and Molly jumped down from her perch to pour coffee for herself and returned to quiet the Dancer. Dashaway Dancer was a typical thoroughbred stallion filled with pomp and attitudes, and now he was even more skittish than usual. The sights and odors of the night were enough to make him nearly unapproachable, but add the storm and he was ready to rear and bolt.

"Easy, big sweetheart," Molly said to Dancer, approaching only from the right as Manny had directed. "Everything is going to be just fine and Molly has some sugar for you. That's it—nice and calm."

Molly showed a sugar cube to the Dancer and now moved it down to eager lips. Dancer took it from her hands. Only two years ago, Dashaway Dancer was an up and coming two-year-old in the mold of War Admiral from the thirties. He had nearly the same majestic appearance. Manuel was an expert on race horses through the ages and, as a three-year-old, Dashaway Dancer had surpassed times set for a mile and a quarter by the likes of Secretariat, Man-O-War, and even War Admiral. His great opportunity to qualify for the Kentucky Derby was squandered when his jockey, Mickey Downey, was accused of race doctoring by pulling in Dancer's reins and digging spurs into the horse's flanks during the last three furlongs of a feature race at Cedar Downs. When Molly's father saw home movies of Dancer being held back, Downey was fired and disqualified from ever riding again. A local reporter discovered Downey's brother had placed serious money on one of the other horses and it was likely Mickey was in on the fix. The picture of Downey on Dancer's back made it look like Dancer had been an accomplice in the crime, but the horse wasn't guilty. Dancer ran other races but never hit the same stride. It was as if his heart was broken and after each new loss, he hung his head and ambled back to the stables. Horse critics said the Dancer had lost a step, but Manny insisted the horse expected his rider to again pull back his reins and had learned to slow purposely as if this was what the jockey wanted him to do. His heart and spirit had been broken. Now he was left to father other horses.

Molly's father had directed the Dancer not be ridden, but Manny confided that one morning when Molly's father was in town, he took Dancer out to the track and, with no one around the track on a misty morning, Dashaway Dancer broke the Cedar Downs' record with one hundred forty pound Manny Gutierrez on his back. Manny explained the average jockey rarely weighs more than one hundred twenty pounds, so there was no real way to know how many seconds he really would have shaved off the track record.

"I never told your father," Manny told Molly, "the truth is it really made no difference. As soon as you have put another horse on that track, Dancer would have thought he was supposed to lose. Mickey kidnapped Dancer's heart. It was a criminal thing to do."

"Why won't my father let him race again?"

"He may some day. He wants Dancer to forget what happened, but at race time a horse never forgets. Dancer expects to be pulled back with spurs in his sides and I don't know if he can forget. That's one of the reasons he has such high hopes for this foal. With Dancer's bloodline and Amazing Grace's temperament, we might have the fastest horse in the nation. What Mickey did was criminal. The Dancer can fly. When I had him out on the track that morning, his mane was back in my face and he was streaking like lightning. He was born to run and any horse with his bloodline will sneak up on all comers. Remember the Dancer didn't get a chance at fame and no one really knows how fast he could have been. Any foal from the Dancer could learn to dash with the wind."

But that was weeks ago, and now the same foal was in terrible danger of having no chance at life at all. Molly sipped her coffee and rubbed at Dancer's perfect forehead star and still the stallion wanted to know what could be happening a few stalls away. Molly tried to move the horse's giant head toward the front of the barn, but each time Amazing Grace whinnied or moved, he immediately turned back to try to see. Molly stroked him and then brushed him with the currycomb hanging from the stall wall, but it was no use. Dashaway Dancer was about to be a father and he seemed to know it.

"Okay," Molly said finally, "I'll go over and take a look and I'll get back with you. How will that be, Dancer? You stay quiet—you hear?"

Molly walked to the corner stall and stoked the Coleman lantern and suddenly the stall was brighter. Her father was still lying in the hay with Amazing Grace's head in his lap and he stroked the side of her face as one would a child. Molly reached down and handed him a second cup of coffee and her father gave her an exhausted look and smiled. Down lower, Manny worked with warm towels and waved off a second cup of coffee.

"We could have her stand up, boss," Manny said. "She can birth standing up."

"Too late now," Marty Grimaldi said. "Grace is calm and ready. We'll be going for it within the hour. Molly, finish your coffee and then go get a bucket of that hot water without burning yourself. I'll need those towel strips and iodine for the stub."

"What stub?"

"The foal will be attached by an umbilical cord. Once it's born and everything comes out, we'll tie off the cord and Manny will snip it and tie it in a knot. If everything somehow goes well, we'll put iodine on the stub so it won't get infected. I'm worried about several things, but we have to take care of the things that we can."

"Tell me, Dad. What are you worried about?"

"I'm worried that you're here, first of all. I don't know what you're going to see."

"I want to be here. If it gets tough, I'll walk away. Just don't chase me away."

"Agreed. I'm trying to tell you all is not well and you need to know that. I know the foal is alive. See how Grace's lower area is pulsing. That's not Grace. It's the foal. Okay, so you know the foal is alive, but the foal is still in distress. Manny knows there's a breech and the foal needs to come out cleanly and smoothly. Then we'll look at the damage."

"Damage?"

"Yes, Molly. This has not been a good birth. Now that the foal is in the canal, we're fairly sure Grace will be okay. The worry now is for the foal. I think at least one leg is tucked under—maybe both—and that's never good. If the foal's legs are broken, there's not much to be done. Understand? The foal has to nurse in the first forty-eight hours and it just can't on broken legs."

"Can't we hold Grace down?"

"Not for two days and the foal needs the mare's antibiotics. It will die without them. We'll just have to wait and see."

"I don't understand. What if the legs are broken? Couldn't we get the milk from Grace and transfer it to the foal? That's possible, right?"

"Honey, it's possible but not wise. There is a right way to do things on a farm. Nature is very funny. As wonderful as Grace is, if she sees the foal is malformed she'll shun it and let it go."

"Let it die?"

"Oh, Molly. Won't you go in the house?"

"You'll let it die?"

"You have to understand when a foal is helpless it's cruel to let it survive."

"You would kill it?"

"Manny would give it a shot."

"And it would die. Is that going to happen?"

"If the foal can't nurse and it's been hurt badly, it's what we have always done. I know how it sounds and it sure isn't what we want to do. I remember when I was a boy we nursed a breech birth and it died as a colt. The other horses never left it alone. I don't know how I can make you understand."

"I do understand and I'm not going in the house," Molly said, "I'm not going in the house. I want to be here in case I can help."

"You understand what might have to be done?"

"Yes."

With that conversation and no more, Molly jumped up to the stall wall and held the lantern so Manny could see. Marty and Manny traded frustrated looks but neither told Molly she couldn't stay. She was determined and there was no use telling her something once she'd made up her mind. Occasionally, Marty looked up at the daughter he adored and she stared down, a pigtail end in her mouth and holding a lantern in her hand, and all the while she said nothing. She had to be so worried and tired and perhaps the easy thing was to send her to the house and to bed. It wouldn't be so easy tomorrow if difficult decisions had to be made. Molly was respected as an equal decision maker in the family and she would be allowed to be present for this one. With Molly, there was no other way.

Now it was nearly four in the morning and every now and then Molly's eyes would ease closed and then snap open. The rain had stopped and it was dank and humid in the barn. Once Molly walked to the door and saw mist rising from the bulrushes next to the pond and the corral and track weren't visible in the mist and dark. On the way back to stall seven, Molly pitched hay in several stalls and now Dashaway Dancer chomped hay and stopped only when he heard sounds from the back of the barn.

"Molly, come here," her father called, "It's time, baby. Either stoke the lantern or go in the house. It's time to decide."

"I stay," Molly said and took the lantern from the stall railing and held it down so Manny could see. Now Amazing Grace strained and her legs splayed open and, looking closely, Molly could see a tiny hoof appear and then suddenly disappear. Molly stared and again a tiny hoof appeared and this time a nose, a muzzle, a white star, eyes, ears, and then a long black neck. "Oh please," Molly said, "Come on, Grace. Please come on."

Marty Grimaldi held Grace's head firmly and now the palomino pushed and reared her head back. Huge arteries in her neck and legs bulged at the surface. The foal emerged inch by inch and Manny held the foal as it came out in increments. Now one leg and the head and neck were visible and Molly panicked when she couldn't see the second leg.

"Push, Grace!" Marty Grimaldi shouted and the palomino strained and Manny dabbed at the foal's eyes and face with a clean white towel. Suddenly there was tremendous sound and movement and a jet-black foal pushed its way into the world. Manny toweled the foal feverishly with towels and now Marty let a giant head loose so Grace could lick and nuzzle her foal. Tears flowed down Molly's face and she tried to see and record everything she'd seen. The foal was beautiful and all the while her father nursed his favorite mare, congratulated her, and now he pushed at her flanks to be sure everything had come out as it should. He saved bags of material for the vet to see and now all attention turned to the foal.

"The legs, Manny?" Marty shouted, "How are the legs?"

"Can't tell yet," Manny answered and he helped the foal nurse while Grace licked at its face and neck, "Can't tell yet, boss. The right leg is fine but I haven't seen the left. Can you keep Grace down just a few minutes?"

"Man, I'm trying. She wants to be up and nursing. I can give you a few minutes."

Molly got her first look at a beautiful foal. He was jet-black like his father but his color was even richer and shinier. This horse was the most gorgeous Molly had ever seen and her eyes were wide and tears flowed steadily down her freckled cheeks.

"Daddy, he's beautiful! Look at him! Welcome to the world, Handsome Boy. You get your milk and get strong. Isn't he handsome?"

"Can't hold her, Manny. Watch the foal. She's getting up."

Powerfully and mightily, Amazing Grace rose, and soon the palomino pulled her one thousand pounds up for the first time in hours. The foal in the hay below, with Manny's help, tried to struggle to its legs. The little horse, no more than one hundred pounds, pushed to its hooves and then stumbled.

"Got a problem, boss," Manny said. "Left front leg is broken."

Molly Grimaldi stared and now she saw what Manny saw. The left leg looked fine at first but now Molly could see it bent in two places—first at the knee and again six or seven inches up. Otherwise the foal was wonderful and beautiful, but this had to be a serious problem. She tried to read her father's face and saw tears in his eyes.

CHAPTER TWO

A Sliver of a Chance

Just before first light, the electricity came back on and now the barn was bathed in light from overhead lamps. Manuel Gutierrez and Marty Grimaldi studied the new foal and Molly watched. Thankfully, Marty had wrapped and splinted the foal's broken left leg and now the tiny horse nursed eagerly while Manny held the withered leg off the ground.

"What happens now, Daddy?"

"Molly, I'm just not sure. The doctor will be here in an hour or two and there's no sense not letting this little guy get the vitamins he needs. I'm going to tell you the truth. A horse with a broken front leg hardly ever gets better, but we'll let the vet make the final call."

"Final call?"

"Look Molly," her father said while he steadied Amazing Grace while her young one fed, "a game legged horse is no account. Sometimes an adult horse can break a leg and respond to care and treatment, but a young one's bones tend to splinter and they can never carry weight. Manny wrapped it just so the doc can take a look, but a no account horse is a luxury we can't afford. Don't you see? A horse takes nearly three years to be ridden and that might double with a horse like this one. Likely even then, he won't handle a rider or be able to pull a wagon. For all your trying, they're no account. Valueless, you understand?"

"So Manny will kill it?"

"No, now that Manny's called the vet and he's on the way over, the vet will make the call. It just doesn't look good. A horse without purpose or value just can't stay on a ranch or farm. Every living thing has to have purpose. You know we've not been able to use Amazing Grace the last six months, and now the whole eleven months of her pregnancy may have been for nothing? And maybe now I'm sorry you saw the foal at all."

"I'll keep my word. I won't act like a selfish kid. The foal just seems perfect in every other way."

"That's the problem. He is. See how his pasterns are bowed just a little for shock absorption when he runs? That's just perfect. See the nostrils flared? Perfect. Hindquarters up and raised, other bones dense and hard, eyes far apart, long sloping shoulders, knees together and straight—he's perfect in every way. I'm just so sorry. He's exactly the right blend of Grace and Dancer and I'd imagine him to get fifteen to seventeen hands high and, as a stallion, every bit of eleven hundred pounds. But that's the problem. A splintered bone now will never support that much weight. He'd be a cripple."

"So really, that's it?" Molly asked, "It's a done deal that you have to put him down?"

"More than likely. This is a beautiful young horse with tremendous promise, but economically he is a disaster."

"I don't understand."

"Farms and ranches operate with crops and animals as money makers or else there wouldn't be farmers and ranchers. A stallion like this one can bring in thousands of dollars. I have to look at the financial side of things. This horse has a wonderful bloodline and maybe he could have run like the Dancer. Even if he would not have raced much, he could have commanded a hefty price in Kentucky and would command a great price for breeding. He won't be able to do either of those things. I don't want to put him down, but keeping a no account horse only worsens the losses we already have. I'll let the vet make the final call, although Manny and I have seen enough in our time to know what that call will be. Do you understand?"

"How can I not understand? I know every plant, person, and animal has to pull weight for a farm to succeed. I know that, Daddy. But should we just give up on him?"

"We're not giving up. We're letting the foal nurse. Manny wrapped the leg. Honey, we're trying to believe in miracles, but beyond seeing a life coming into the world, there aren't many miracles on a farm. Most farm miracles come from hard work and planning. Ranchers and farmers see life and death every day. Go to the grocery store and see all the miracles farmers and ranchers bring to market. The meat section Mrs. Brown shops were once live animals on a farm. The vegetables Mrs. Smith selects were planted and watered and nursed by farmers. City people will never understand farm miracles. No one sees when the farmer fails—just the farmer who has lost his product. Maybe one in a thousand thoroughbreds gets to run in a major race and only three of those running win, place, or show. The rest earn nothing on race day, but money was spent. Think of the horses that never had the chance Dancer had. Their owners lost money. We will lose money here. We did everything right. Things just didn't go the way we hoped. Mother Nature can be very kind and very unforgiving. Before you were born, we had a tornado come through here that destroyed all the crops, destroyed over two hundred orange trees, and killed seventeen of our best horses and steers. No one gave us a penny. Several years later we had six mares foal the same season and we sold five of the horses for more than we owed. The sixth horse was Dashaway Dasher."

"Wow."

"The best part is Dr. Cable told us exactly the right horse to keep. He examined all six colts and then just pointed at Dancer and walked away. Dashaway won enough in races to save this farm. Even after he lost his nerve, he had made money fathering horses in three counties. Dr. Cable made the right call."

"Why is that the best part?"

"Because Dr. Cable will be the one to make the right call this morning. Manny called him instead of Evers because we want the man with the most knowledge to decide what we should do. See, we haven't given up. Cable will tell us if we should. He was right about the Dancer and he'll be right again this morning. Can you live with what he says?"

"I suppose," Molly said, watching Manny cradling the foal's left leg as it nursed. "I just want to vote that if there is a sliver of a chance to save this horse, I'll do everything to save him. Everything. I mean it, Dad. I'll stay out here day and night. I'll feed him, exercise him, pamper him, and love him."

"What about when you go back to school in the fall?"

"I'll wake up early and stay up late. If he has to die, I will understand. I just want you to understand that if prayers and efforts can create miracles on a farm, I want to be part of one."

"How old are you?"

"You know I'm twelve."

"Going on about thirty-five," her father said, "You are an amazing girl. You are my miracle on this farm. I'm sorry you've had to go through so much."

"Just let me have a voice."

"Yes, ma'am."

"We shouldn't name him yet, should we?"

"Do you think we should, Molly?"

"No, not until we hear what the doctor says."

"Then that's what we'll do."

It wasn't a long wait. Just before nine in the morning Manny walked Amazing Grace out to the corral and yelled back toward the barn that the vet just turned into the Grimaldi driveway. Dashaway Dasher got his first glance at his son and whinnied his approval as the foal was moved to a fresh stall. The foal slept now and Molly covered him with a blanket while her father went out to greet the vet.

Doctor August Cable was something of a celebrity in the Ocala area. Back in the days when Ocala had more ranches and horse farms anywhere south of Kentucky, 'Augie' Cable was the only vet in the area. Even though he was now close to seventy, no one would ever make a medical decision without the insight of Doc Cable. Now his Bronco bounced in the sloppy ruts the rain had caused and soon Molly could hear Doc and her father discussing the events of the night.

"Aw," Augie Cable said in his familiar way of starting sentences. "You know I'd have been here if the phones had been working. Grace looks none the worse for wear. You save everything for me?"

"I did," Molly heard her father say. "This was a tough one, Augie. My little girl watched the whole thing."

"Aw, was that a good idea, Martin?"

"It was at the time. How did I know things were going to go the way they did? Manny told you, right? Actually, I needed her. She made coffee and brought cookies and I don't know how she got the water out here from the house. She's afraid of lightning and had to dance through all night. She even helped me iodine the cord clips. She was a trooper all night."

"She needs to get some rest."

"No way was she going to bed until she hears what you have to say."

"Aw, and what makes you think she'll sleep if I have bad things to say?"

"She'll sleep sooner or later, Augie. I can't have you feeling like a bad guy. You say what you need to say and I'll deal with Molly."

"Yes, you will, Martin. You say the left leg is broken?"

"Pretty much all the way across, Augie. It was just hanging until Manny and I taped it so it could nurse. He hasn't been allowed to put any weight on it, but I know he couldn't if he tried. How can we tell a foal not to bounce and run? He has his daddy's temperment and he wants to move. The moment he puts weight on it, he'll crumble. He doesn't seem to be in pain, but he might be no account. You ready to look at him?"

"Aw, no," Augie said. "Send the little girl out and let me talk to her first."

"I'm already here," Molly said, slipping from behind the door. "I guess I was kind of listening to you two."

"Molly Grimaldi," Doc Cable shouted, "you come right here and let me look at you. You're beautiful. I haven't seen you in so long. What are you now—around seventeen?"

"Hi, Doctor Cable," Molly said, hugging an old friend, "You know I'm just twelve. What are you now—around thirty-five?"

"Beautiful and smart," Cable said. "Yep, I just turned thirty-five a few decades ago. Actually, I look pretty good for a man a hundred and six years old. I hear we have a new friend."

"I hope we do."

"I heard what your father said, but we know he doesn't know what he's talking about. Come over here on this bench with me and tell me what you saw. Marty, you go take care of the foal. I need to hear from an expert what she had to deal with last night. Sit down here, Molly. Tell me what you saw. Marty, go do what I told you."

"Shouldn't we just go look at the foal?" Molly asked.

"No, we should gather information, Molly. Now, tell me what happened."

"Well, the power went out around nine and Manny went down to quiet the horses and then he came back and told Daddy that Grace was ready."

"Yeah?"

"Well, we all went out there and got the lanterns and blankets and all that stuff and everything was going fine and then Daddy said the foal was breeched."

"This is important, Molly," Doc Cable said, holding Molly's hands in his own. "What time was it when your dad said the foal was breeched? Was it early in the delivery or late?"

"It was about two in the morning. I just came back from the house and the wind up clock said it was one-thirty when I left."

"Was Amazing Grace standing or lying down when the foal came?"

"She was down in the hay with my dad holding her."

"Did the foal come out slowly or all at once?"

"First slowly and, when he started coming, all at once."

"What did you notice about his legs?"

"The right leg came out with the head, but we didn't see the left one at first. I think it was tucked under him."

"See, your father wouldn't have seen that," Doc Cable said. "What that means is we have the break we can see but we may have other damage as well. Okay, let me explain that part. The leg that's broken is obvious, but the joint above it may be twisted too. See how important that is? We could look at one area and miss another. I want to save this horse just like you do, but we both need to understand that each leg on an adult stallion may have to support three hundred pounds. I'm going to need your help to make the right decision."

"You want my help?"

"Can't do without it. If you really want to help me, I need for you to think with your head and not your heart. Do you know what I mean by that?"

"I think so," Molly answered, "I shouldn't want the foal to live no matter what. I should want the foal to live only if it has a chance of a good life. My brain would tell the truth, but maybe my heart wouldn't."

"I couldn't have said it better myself. For you to be involved, you have to act like my assistant. You have to act like this is someone else's farm and someone else's horse, and you have to decide what's best for the horse and the farm. Can you do that, Molly?"

"I'm not sure I can, but I want to try. Why isn't this more up to my dad?"

"Your dad will listen and agree with a final decision, but I wanted to talk to you because my decision will be based on things you can do that your father can't. This is between you and me."

"What could I do that my father can't?"

"Honey, your father has a farm to run. He can't give time to an injured foal even if he wanted to—he just can't. He has the cows, the other horses, the orange grove, and the million and one things it takes to keep a place running. I won't give false hope. This foal sounds like it is in very grave trouble. At the very least, it will need a lot of daily care. Your dad doesn't have time for that and that will color his decision. Molly, you must understand I will make a medical decision, not an emotional one."

"I understand."

"Now, let's go in the barn and meet a new life," Doc Cable said.

Even though Doctor August Cable was seventy years old, he still wore a cowboy hat and boots. Clearly his riding days were long over, but he wasn't quite willing to hang up the look of a cowboy. He was about five feet six inches tall and now had a paunchy stomach, and looked more leprechaun than cowboy. His hands were wrinkled and sprinkled with age spots that seemed to multiply each time he came to visit. He had sea blue eyes and white eyebrows that needed trimming, but his voice was always calming and no one in the county knew more about horses.

Molly's father liked to tell a story about a young colt that simply refused to be examined. The young horse was too feisty to be settled down long enough for the doctor to get a good look at him. Suddenly, Doc Cable stared into the colt's right eye and swatted the horse's ears as hard as he could. "Now, are you going to listen to me?" Doc shouted. The colt froze. Every time after that, Doctor Cable would pull on the horse's ears before an examination and the horse would remember. Doc wanted that horse to know he remembered, too. Doc and the colt became great friends, but Marty Grimaldi insisted the colt would always pull back his ears the moment he saw Doc's wagon coming up the drive. There was no one on the planet who would make a fairer decision about the new life in the barn and Molly knew he talked to her first to assure her that he would be fair. Molly followed him into the barn and resolved she would agree with whatever Doc said, and, if there were tears, she'd save them for her room. If Doc said there was no other choice, there was no other choice. Doc loved and understood horses as much as anyone ever could.

Cable wasted no time. In seconds, he tossed his cowboy hat over a stall post and he was down in the hay with Grace's foal. Molly could only see the bald spot on Doc's head and she wished she could see the expressions on his face as he started the examination at the horse's head, touching and petting the foal with perfect and loving hands. He kissed the side of the foal's face and felt along the neck with his hands. He moved along the withers and backbone and then he listened to the heart and lungs. He examined the back legs from hips to hooves and now he felt along the stomach. Doc seemed to be avoiding the front legs. Molly judged the foal was developing trust in new hands on him.

"Okay, Marty," Doc said, rising to his feet. "You and Manny get this foal up on its feet and get crossties on either side of the stall. I want the wrappings off—good job by the way, and I want Molly to push so he favors his right side. Aw, Marty, this is a beautiful horse. Hindquarters are perfect, head straight and erect, pasterns excellent; ears perfect swivel, eyes piercing and strong, shoulders strong and fluid. Only the Dancer has fetlocks with this angle—nice. Aw, Marty, this is a nice horse."

Molly was encouraged by all the things Doc said, but he had said nothing about the left leg. Now he examined the right leg. He held both hands around the lower leg just above the hoof and moved up an inch at a time all the way to the horse's face and muzzle before starting down the left leg. Molly held her breath as Doc moved slowly and soon he reached the point of the break. The foal pulled back, but Doc held steady and gently bent the leg at the knee and returned to the area seven or so inches up the femur bone. With hands as sensitive as a surgeon's, Cable moved his fingers all the way around the bone. He eased the leg back to the ground and now he rubbed his face and just stared ahead. Again, he lifted the leg, gently bent it at the knee, and returned to the troubled area. Marty and Manny watched as Doc circled his baby finger all the way around the bone. Each time Doc shook his head Molly was sure he was about to speak, but each time he said nothing.

"Aw," Doc said finally, "I want liniment and new dressings. We're going to bind this until we can go outside and talk. Manny, I want this horse to nurse again—antibiotics are really important the first forty-eight hours. Aw, this is a mess. Molly, watch exactly how I do this: first the liniment, then the gauze, now a tight wrap, see—don't worry how tight— wrap cloth like this, and finish with plastic wrap. Think you can do that?"

"I think I can do what you did," Molly said quietly. "If I can help, I'll do anything."

"Then be creative," Doc said without explanation. "Now Manny, get Grace in here and be careful she doesn't reject this foal. I don't want Grace to see this foal is damaged right away. She might do the wrong thing."

"What do you mean?" Molly asked.

"Your dad will explain later. Let's go and talk this out. Molly, if you'll make coffee I won't say a word until you get back. I keep my promises. Now, go do that."

"What do we have here, Doc?" Marty asked the moment Molly ran toward the house.

"What we have is a father who didn't listen to what I just said. We will wait for your daughter like I said we would."

"You sure you don't want to tell me first?"

"Aw, Marty. You need to respect that little girl and keep all your promises. You'll want her to keep hers later and you should show her how that's done. We wait for Molly."

"I understand. I just thought maybe you would want me to know first."

"Why?"

"Never mind. I got the message. Let me go check the Dancer and feed the cows and I'll be right back. If Molly comes out, she won't even see us together."

Totally exhausted, Marty walked zigzag toward the corral with his filthy jeans rubbing together. He stopped a couple of times to hitch them up. Doc watched Marty move toward the corral. He had known this man since he was a boy, and now had the utmost respect for him. Molly's mother Denise died after a long and valiant battle with breast cancer and the whole time Marty never cried or complained. Now left with his pre-teen daughter and trying to save his failing farm, Marty Grimaldi never complained.

Managing Molly, the orange groves, the horses, the cattle, and with only Manuel to help with a thousand chores, Marty was a man who was very tired. He didn't need more bad news. Marty was forty-two, graying slightly at the temples, more than six feet tall and still rock-muscled. Women in town and at church figured Marty was handsome and available. But he wasn't available to any woman. Although Denise passed, Marty was still married to his farm, the chores, and his daughter, who needed her father more than ever.

Doc Cable watched Marty stumble where cows waited and he tossed hay in the hoppers, patted the flanks of three cows, and walked bowlegged back toward the barn. He was tired. There was little rest for a farmer on his own. Doc wished he had better news. Molly arrived with coffee and she and her father sat with Doc at an old picnic table that had been used for everything from cleaning fish to Sunday barbecues.

Mysteriously, now Doc looked his age. His wrinkles had become creases and his blue eyes seemed to be as gray as a beach sky when a dark cloud comes and sends beachgoers scurrying back to their cars. Doc rubbed his chin and ran his fingers through white hair. He seemed to start to speak and then stopped as if the words were not arranged in the proper order. Molly crossed her arms to keep her hands from shaking. She slid closer to her father. There was a storm coming and she was determined Doc should not see her cry.

24

"Aw, Molly and Marty," Doc said finally, "this is a hard time for me and soon will be a hard time for you. I've been a vet forty-three years and I have seen so much. I've seen situations where there are no right answers and yours is one of those situations. If you'll indulge an old man a story or two, I'll come around to the point. This is very bad, Marty. It's bad because there are answers, but none of them are good. Molly, we talked before and now we will talk to the point."

"Yes?" Molly asked.

"Yes, there is much to be said, but let me start this way: Did you know the all time speed record at the Kentucky Derby was one minute fifty-nine seconds set by Secretariat?"

"What's that have to do with anything, Doc?" Marty asked.

"Everything," Doc answered. "Now if you'll close your mouth and open your ears, I'll explain. Aw, Secretariat was a fine stallion. He and War Admiral were the fastest horses I've ever seen. When Secretariat set that record, I got to thinking. You do the math, but if he ran the mile and a quarter in less than two minutes, that's over thirty miles per hour not counting the time to build up to top speed. Can you imagine how many times his feet hit the ground going that fast? Get in a car and go thirty-five miles per hour and just watch how fast the ground races past and then imagine a man and horse at that speed. Secretariat is coaxed into the starting gate and 'Boom' the gates open and fifteen horses explode onto the track and in seconds mud is flying everywhere. He accelerates pulling with his front legs and thrusting with back legs. He expels air from his mouth and his nostrils flare taking fresh air to lungs, mane and tail flap in the wind, whips crackle, and the jockeys shout like maniacs. Secretariat feels heels in his flanks and he stretches to maximum, arteries filled with blood, hooves digging and thundering, eyes fixed and dilated—thunder and lightning. Don't think the horses don't know. They do. It's man against man and horse against horse and the jockeys, their fannies in the air, hang close to ears and plead for even more speed. Secretariat hears the voice and he stretches almost out his skin and his heart beats out of rhythm. There is but one thing: to win. Man and beast become one with the earth and they blend with the universe for an exquisite moment and now Secretariat hears the crowd and pulls his ears back. He pumps and pumps, legs flying willy-nilly, pushing and crowding, trying to breathe and he thrusts his nose and chest through an imaginary line and he knows he has won. It is all over in two minutes, and fourteen horses lose.

"Wow, Doc," Marty said, "I could see what you were saying."

"Then you can see the story has a point. Once those gates fly open a world of speed and Mother Nature takes over. Every person in the stands expects horse and rider to be in perfect condition, but that's never the truth. The race tells the truth. I've known of horses that had heart attacks and still finish the race before they fall over dead. I saw a race where a horse finished on three legs with the fourth shattered in pieces. His leg was broken but his heart was not. I heard a story of a Scottish jockey who was dead on his horse's back, but the horse finished the race. Do you get it? The race is the ultimate competition and no one but horses and jockeys know the truth. A thoroughbred will run until he drops. To run is a horse's reason to exist as much as a fish swims and a flower blooms. A thoroughbred denied running with the wind lives an empty life. I know. I was a jockey."

"Could you be a little clearer on what we're talking about today?" Marty asked.

"I'm being very clear. Here's the deal: your foal is the result of perfect breeding. Your palomino mare runs with endurance and the Dancer runs with blazing speed. The combination in this foal could have made him a champion. You saw me examine him. He's perfect in every way and now that works against him and his survival."

"How?"

"He can survive. That bone, with Molly's care each and every day, could heal enough to be a decent riding horse. You'd have to shackle him like they do with trotters. He should never be allowed to run full blast. He should never extend the way Secretariat did. I examined that leg as best I could without an x-ray and the good news is the break seems clean. It must have happened just seconds before he was born—a quick snap. The bone isn't splintered and that is good news."

"The bad news?" Molly asked.

"Aw," Doc Cable said, lighting his pipe, "The bone is broken almost all the way through and, no matter what we do, that bone will never be right. Never. He might run a hundred times and crumble on the one hundred first. That's disaster for him and anyone on his back. That chance should never be taken."

"Tell me what to do, Doc," Marty said.

"You know a car rarely goes as fast as it can, but a car doesn't have a heart. Remember when that idiot jockey held Dancer back and wouldn't let him run? It broke that stallion's heart and spirit. He's never been the same, has he? A rider is in control at the beginning and end of a race and holds on for dear life in between—the horse is dancing on the wind and doesn't know or care someone is on his back. Your horse has the bloodline of champions and he'll run the very first chance he gets."

"And?"

"And the leg will break in the exact spot it did today. Molly, remember how I told you each leg supports about three hundred pounds of weight? In a full gallop, we just don't know. We do know front legs support two thirds of a horse's weight—more than the back legs, but how much a leg supports in full gallop is much more. Those legs hit the ground again and again and they pull to gain more speed. That's why I told you about Secretariat. I don't know what else to say. We have a choice here. I just think an eagle that can't soar is just a bird. A toothless tiger is a housecat. I'm not sure, though, that a racehorse that can't run is even a horse."

"So you're saying it's best we put him down?" Marty asked.

"I'm saying you and Molly should give it some thought. You'll break his heart and he's sure to break yours. I'll guarantee I could be wrong, but, like I said, I've seen everything. About thirty years ago, Henry Cheever down the road took a chance with a horse like this one. He seemed fine after a year of close training. They found a jockey less than a hundred pounds to ride him. That crazy horse won six races before he crumbled. If that wasn't bad enough, when he went down two other horses went down with him. It was a disaster."

"What happened?" Molly asked.

"I won't say," Doc Cable said and he wiped at his eyes as if he could still see what he couldn't say.

"Can I ask a question?" Molly said.

"I want you to make a good decision. Ask any question."

"When we talked about saving the foal, I said I'd do anything. You said I could 'be creative.' What did you mean?"

"That's a very good question, Molly. Okay, let me answer this way. Back in the early 1930s a knobby-kneed foal was born. Even his owner called him a 'masterpiece of faulty construction' and he was sold for eight thousand dollars. That wasn't much for a horse that was bred to be a champion. His new trainer, Tommy Smith was his name, believed everyone was wrong about that horse so he took him to Detroit to train him. No one paid attention because everyone said the colt was no account. His jockey got the horse a spotted dog named Pumpkin and they became great friends. Part of their creative training program involved never waking up the horse while he was sleeping. They found a broken down one-eyed jockey named George Wolf and that man talked to that horse as much as he rode him. It was the craziest training program for a no account horse that there ever was. Do you know the name of that horse, Molly?"

"No."

"You, Marty?"

"Should I?"

"Yes, you should. Ever hear of a horse called 'Seabiscuit?'"

"You're kidding," Marty said.

"Nope," Doc said, smiling at the memory. "At that time there was a horse named War Admiral that was said to be the fastest horse that ever lived in the 50,000 years of horses being on the planet. War Admiral won The Triple Crown in 1937 and no one could beat him."

"What's 'The Triple Crown?'"

"Come on, Molly," Marty said, "The Kentucky Derby, The Preakness, and The Belmont Stakes are three races held in spring and, because they're different lengths, it's hard to win all three. Doc is saying War Admiral won all three."

"In one hundred twenty-nine years, only eleven horses have won The Triple Crown. Anyway, the owners of Seabiscuit challenge War Admiral to a match race—only one horse against the other with the winner taking all the money."

"Seabiscuit won?" Molly asked.

"Sure did. Everyone was shocked except the owner, the jockey, and, especially, Seabiscuit. People said two crippled old men won that race."

"So you say there's a chance?"

"In a million," Doc said, "Molly, you heard what I said?"

"But you also said if a person was creative, there is a chance. You said that, right?"

"But Doc also said he'd vote to put the horse down," Marty Grimaldi said, "Did you hear the part about breaking the horse's heart and ours too? Did you hear how the horse could crumble—maybe even with you on his back?"

"I wouldn't be on his back unless it was totally safe. I wouldn't hurt the horse or me."

"Pretty girl," Augie Cable said, "this is a very difficult situation."

"You also said you couldn't be sure either way."

"I did say that, but I also said it's a million-to-one shot."

"Isn't that what Seabiscuit was?"

"Yes, but that was with the best and most creative training of all time."

"Until now," Molly said.

"What?" Marty Grimaldi asked.

"I already have creative ideas. Please let me try."

"And if you fail?"

"Give me until Christmas and if the horse isn't sound, I'll let you take him away. Yes, I know what will happen when you take him away."

"Doc?"

"Molly, listen. This is an extensive and expensive decision. You will have to do this because your father can't. Do you realize how much money and time could be lost?"

"Doctor," Molly said, sounding very grown up, "do you realize how much money and time has already been lost?"

"She's got you there, Doc," Marty said. "She's as stubborn as her mother. Molly, a little girl cannot do all you say you can do. A woman cannot do all you want to do. Heck, most men couldn't possibly do all you want to do."

"This woman can do it if you'll let me. I'll sometimes need your help."

"Doc?"

"You meant what you said about Christmas?"

"I won't accept a horse with a broken heart," Molly said.

"You just lost a summer, Miss Molly," her father said.

"You mean it?"

"Will I regret it?" her father asked.

"You'll never regret that you let me try."

"Doctor Cable?" Molly asked, touching the old man's shoulder.

"I know horses, but I believe in you. Just do the right thing at Christmas."

"You'll come out and help me decide?"

"Yes."

"Now, can I name him?"

"I suppose," her father said.

"Don't get mad, Doctor Cable," Molly said. "But I'd like to call him 'Handsome Augie.' Would that make you mad?"

"You'd name him that?" Doc asked.

"Would that be okay?"

Doctor August Cable buried his face in his hands.

CHAPTER THREE

Secret Potions, Magic Leaves, and Doc Cable

At one time Ocala, Florida was known as 'horse country,' but now the Grimaldi farm was one of the few surviving family farms. Land that once supported horses and cattle had become housing subdivisions. Family farms had been sold to big company orange growers or companies that grew organic tomatoes that would be marketed to a major ketchup company.

The whole of Florida is much different from the brochures that advertise Disney World or resorts along the ocean. The area of Florida devoted to tourists covers only the first five or six inland miles of the coastline. The majority of Florida belongs to farms or alligators. Florida ranks fourth in the nation in numbers of horses, many of them in Ocala. Huge companies and wealthy ranchers now own most of the farms, but there are still farmers like the Grimaldis.

The foal was four days old now and every day Manny and Molly held Amazing Grace steady while 'Augie' nursed. He had already developed the habit of standing three-legged while he nursed. He loved the calcium enriched hay Molly added to his diet and he ate it as fast as he could. Molly mixed water and blended carrots and apples into a messy liquid. Augie loved it too, and pushed his nose to the bottom of the pail to get every last drop.

Doc Cable had worried the foal wouldn't eat or that Grace might not allow nursing, but these were never problems. The foal had a tremendous appetite and Molly had to be careful not to over feed him. The big problem was that Augie wanted to run and play. This could not be allowed. Molly decided to walk him four times a day in the chute that years ago was used to line up cattle for branding. It was a hundred feet long and was really a long and straight tunneled fence about five feet wide that made cows walk in single file to face a branding iron at the end. Along the way, cowboys perched on the fence would inject the cows with vaccinations and vitamins. This was the easiest and best way to keep track of which cattle had been vaccinated and branded and how many more had to pass through the line. It was perfect for exercising Augie. He had to walk straight. With Molly walking in front of him, he couldn't try to run. She held a soft cloth rope around the foal's neck and he walked with her. Every now and then Augie would try to rush past her, but Molly blocked him like a football player. In the morning, Molly took him through the run three times back and forth, at noon four times, before dinner three more times, and, just before dark, four final times. Altogether, Augie's walking sessions were almost three thousand feet a day. Molly increased it by eight hundred feet, one extra lap each session, every fourth day. She used a notebook to chart each walk and note Augie's progress after each session. Mostly Molly walked backward and faced the foal as they walked. If she saw even a hint of a limp, she ended the session. There was no textbook about how to train a lame foal.

After the first two weeks, Molly felt her own calves and thighs becoming stronger, so she reasoned the exercises had to be good for the foal. Augie would become so excited the moment Molly picked up the rope he had to be crowded into a corner of his stall so he wouldn't become too feisty and hurt his leg. Each time Manny zoomed by on the tractor or her father cantered past exercising one of the adult horses, both men would salute and shout, "How's it goin', General Grimaldi?" Molly would smile and give the thumbs-up. Then she and Augie would start another lap. At the end of the third week, each session ended with the reward of an apple or a carrot. Augie nuzzled Molly reminding her it was time for a reward.

One morning in early July, Molly saw a familiar Bronco navigating the potholes in the long driveway. Doc Cable bounced in the front seat each time the Bronco bounced in the ruts created by the most recent storm. Molly waved from the chute as she and Augie finished a final lap. A cowboy hat waved back from the side window and Doc shouted, "I come to see my grandbaby!"

"Hi, Doc!" Molly shouted back and she led Augie to the small parking area.

"You leading a dog or a horse?" Doc asked as he hugged Molly. "Well, look at you and your buddy. Aw, he looks fine, Molly. You walking him every day?"

"Four times every day," Molly said. "When it rains we walk inside the barn."

"Let's go there now. I brought my bag. We're going to give him a booster shot and some new antibiotics I just got. He looks fine, Molly. What a beautiful young horse. He's getting darker and the star whiter. He is handsome."

"Handsome Augie Grimaldi," Molly said. She watched as the foal pushed his nose in Doc's face and then moved down to the old man's pocket. "What'cha got in there, Doc?" she asked.

"Aw, ain't nothin' but a sugar cube for my grandson," Doc said. He held his hand flat and Augie's lips tickled at his hand and a sugar cube was gone, "You lead him with that rope like a dog and he follows you?"

"That's all he knows."

"No bit or harness or anything?"

"He doesn't know he's supposed to have one."

"I see," Doc said. "No, actually, I don't see. I don't guess I've ever seen that before. Doesn't he rear back on the rope?"

"Not so far."

"I see," Doc said and he rubbed his hand over his chin. "Let's give him a physical and you can show me how you have been dressing that leg."

"He's a really fine horse," Molly said. "After I cook breakfast and get lunch ready for Daddy and Manny, I spend most of the day with Augie. We do our morning walk, we have our morning talk, and then I redress the leg."

"Morning talk?"

"Well, every morning I tell him how wonderful he is. I tell him all about Secretariat and Seabiscuit. I have their pictures in Augie's stall so he sees them and I tell him he has to look and act like a champion. Then we have our hay and spinach and we have our brushing and carrots and apples."

"Did you say 'spinach'?"

"Worked for Popeye," Molly said. "Maybe it'll work for a horse."

"Okay," Doc said. "Spinach, huh? I guess it won't hurt him at all. I said for you to be creative and you're doing that. It looks like something's working. His coat is shiny and his eyes are as bright as fireflies."

"That's good, huh?"

"That's very good," Doc said. "Now, let's take a look here. I wish I was as handsome as this horse. He sure is perfect. Look at how the muscles are knotting already—don't believe I've ever seen that."

"We're up to eight thousand feet a day."

"What?"

"I measure it. We walk eight thousand feet a day."

"How would you know that?"

"I can't let him in with the other horses, even Grace. I'm afraid they'll get rough with him, so we walk the old cattle chute. It's ninety-seven feet long and I measure it that way. I don't want that left leg hitting the ground too many times, so I keep a log. If he has a bad day, we cut back. I think I need him to walk on it every day, but I watch to see if he stutter-steps."

"Does he?"

"He did the first two weeks, but not lately. He gets tired on the last walk sometimes, but I think he's doing okay."

"Aw, Molly, he's doing more than okay. What have you been putting on this leg?"

"Why, is it doing badly?"

"No, it feels really strong. I can still feel the ring, but not like before. What the heck you been putting on this leg?"

"Come here and I'll show you," Molly said, using crossties to mobilize Augie in his stall. "He needs to rest now. Do you know he sleeps like that? Sometimes his eyes are still a little open, but he's sleeping. Like Seabiscuit, I don't wake him."

"I see," Doc said, smiling widely, "Ever think about being a vet, Molly?"

"Lately, I have," Molly said and now she took Doc into an empty stall. On the floor and on the shelf of the stall were bottles and lotions and plants. A long steel pot filled with the foulest smelling goop Doc had ever seen sat in the middle of the floor. Doc held his nose and knelt next to the container.

"Molly, this smells horrible. What all you got in here?"

"Everything I could think of," Molly answered. She stirred the potion with the business end of what used to be a shovel. "I make it once a week. I try to get the recipe the same each time."

"The recipe?"

"You said be creative. I have all kinds of great stuff in here. I know it smells really bad, but I think it's working. You know how the Indians would make a poultice to draw out impurities and make wounds heal and bones get stronger?"

"I guess so."

"Well, I got everything except the kitchen sink in here. I start with mud like the Indians did and then I mix in your liniment and some Bengay."

"Bengay?"

"That's what you use for sore muscles and bones, right? Well, that's right, isn't it?'

"I suppose."

"Okay, then. Next I mix in lots and lots of aloe juice from the big plant behind the house. Then I put in the potato peels to bring out the toxins. I juice them up so he's not walking around with peels hanging off him. Then, I add leaves all ground up, onions, Vaseline, a little axle grease, and some tube stuff from the medicine cabinet."

"Starting to sound like a salad. What's that other smell? You know, that really strong smell. I've smelled it before, but I can't place it."

"Oh yeah!" Molly shouted, beaming now. "That's the most important thing. It's Vapo-rub!"

"Vapo-rub?"

"Yeah, I remember when I was sick with a chest cold when I was little, my mom would rub that stuff all over my neck and chest and it like worked inside and made me breathe better. Somehow that stuff gets inside the skin. So I was thinking that could like open Augie's pores so the other things could work."

"I don't know if there's a medical explanation for all that, but if it works you could market 'Molly's Salve' and make a million dollars. If smelling bad means working good, this stuff should work miracles. What do you do—just slop it on the leg?"

"Yep, three times a day. The mud is nice and cool and then all those ingredients start working. You know. I put a good layer of goo on and then I let it get almost dry, put on the bandages, and then another layer of goo. When that dries, we go out walking."

"Gotta tell you, Molly, that's the craziest concoction I've ever seen, but I'm not going to tell you it won't work. You have some good ingredients there with the aloe and liniment and I've heard potato skins do cause chemical reactions. Just look at how quickly they turn brown. That's a chemical reaction. You keep doing what you're doing, honey. You have any time for anything else?"

"Don't want to do anything else. I don't have many friends around here. I cheat and watch my soaps while I clean house in the afternoon, but mostly I like to spend time with Augie. He's really funny."

"What does he do?"

"He actually snorts around to find the spinach in his feed and I dip his vitamins in water and then roll them in sugar. He thinks they're treats and he'll follow me around to get one. Then the other day I took him to see his father run. Manny was running Dancer around the track and the faster they went the more Augie got excited. Then Manny brought the Dancer to the other side of the fence and the horses took turns snorting and smelling each other. Dancer was so interested and Augie stood really still and Dancer got all excited. You think maybe he knew Augie was his son?"

"It's so hard to know what a stallion knows. I know they can smell a female from an incredibly long distance away and can find sugar in the smallest nook or cranny. Smells and touches are essential to horses and I think they can memorize certain odors. So, yes, I think Dancer knows this foal is special. He's never paid attention to one before, so his interest seems significant."

"You know, I think he knows because Dancer doesn't like other horses and in the corral he's mean to the smaller ones. Dad says when the Dancer was racing, he always had to be stopped from trying to bite the other horses. I know that's because he's thoroughbred. But this time with Augie he was so curious and so gentle. Manny was worried when their faces were together but Dancer was feeling with his lips and never flashed his teeth. His ears never laid back and he was pushing and nudging and Augie was pushing and nudging right back. Augie was so cute. It was like Augie was impressed that his dad was so magnificent and he was trying to be just like him."

"Aw, Molly," Doc said, "you're doing a fine job. We're on new ground here, so I won't say anyone could do better than you are. In the old days, especially on small ranches and farms, a horse like Augie would have never been allowed to come this far. That makes you a trailblazer. Has Augie been allowed to run yet?"

"You said he couldn't run. He sure wants to—more and more—I try to walk as fast as I can, but he wants more."

"So, let's give him more."

"What?"

"Molly, it's time to find out how 'Molly Meds' are working out. Let's take him out to the small corral. I'll get your dad while you get him ready. I want you to take him to the center of the corral and wait for us. Then we'll leave him alone and see what he does. Most foals are running by the second day. Maybe that bone will let yours run now. We'll station ourselves in the ring and the moment he stumbles we'll grab him."

"Doc, I'm afraid."

"Be afraid not to let him run. He's a horse. He needs a life beyond you. I'm not sure what will happen now, but if we don't test it now, the leg will surely fail later. You see that, don't you? You can't walk him through the chute the rest of his life."

"I guess I know that. A real vet would know that."

"Did you ever meet my daughter?"

"I didn't know you had one."

"Yes, I do," Doc said. "Her name is Karen and she's out in Colorado learning to be a vet just like her old man. There's a great school out there and she's learning everything from horseshoeing to successful breeding. Anyway, just like your mom and dad did with you, one day we took the training wheels off her bike and 'Boom' down she went. She wanted us to put the training wheels back on, but no way. Up she goes again and down she goes again. Then off she goes and she doesn't even look back. A few years later I put her in a car all by herself and off she goes and doesn't even look back. Now she's twenty-nine and all the way in Colorado. You starting to understand?"

"I understand but I think it's too early."

"Would it be better if one day Augie breaks into a run and I'm nowhere around?"

"I'll get his rope."

Several minutes later with Doc, Manny, and her father waiting at the corral, Molly led her foal out to the small corral. Augie headed for the chute, but this time Molly pulled him toward the corral and led him to the center. Augie looked confused and Molly kissed at the side of his face and fed him a small carrot.

"Now," Doc said, "ease the rope from his neck and slowly walk away. You might have to come sit on the fence. Do it really slowly, Molly."

"Is this a good idea?" Molly asked.

"Some ideas don't have the luxury of being clearly good or bad," her father said. "Take off the rope, Molly."

Molly rubbed her horse's ears, took his lead rope, and hid it behind her back. She walked awkwardly toward her father's position at the split rail fence.

Suddenly the foal looked lonely and fragile standing alone in the middle of the corral. Augie looked confused that Molly should be so far away. He pawed at the turf and looked over at Doc. He raised his head and scanned all three standing at different points along the fence. No one moved and Handsome Augie now surveyed more open space than he'd ever seen in front of him. Now he walked slowly in a straight line directly toward Molly. He nuzzled at her stomach and Molly patted his neck and turned him back to the center of the corral. For several minutes, a foal that seemed tinier than his one hundred pounds, walked further and further away from Molly. He seemed to be discovering freedom a moment at a time. There was no rope around his neck and no straight line to follow and now he held his head up and pranced to see if anyone would stop him. His legs seemed straight and strong. His pace quickened to a slow trot. Augie looked surprised that no fence bound him and his legs moved faster and he began to make circles around the corral.

Molly held her breath. Now all four humans moved off to the side and smiled as a month-old horse zoomed by again and again. Augie was incredibly fast and he never broke rhythm. His strides became faster and he held his head higher. Suddenly Molly began to cry. For her it was like watching her own child's first steps and her father hugged her as Handsome Augie preened and danced his way across the corral. From his first moment on earth, he had never been this far away from Molly. Suddenly, he stopped. Then he walked slowly toward Molly. He nuzzled Molly's face until she laughed. Then he whirled off for the other side of the corral and shook out his mane. He was exhausted.

"What now, Doc?" Molly asked.

"That sure was one of the sweetest things I've ever seen. It's clear to me that bone doesn't bother the foal now, but I don't know if you can ever absolutely trust it. You sure did a fine job. You keep on putting that junk on his leg and keep adding calcium to his feed, and then, I still just don't know. I don't want anything on his back for a few more months and that'll give him a chance to be bridle broken. You don't have to walk the chute with him anymore. He's ready to be loose in the corral, but I don't want him to be alone in it. Something could happen that you don't see. He'll strengthen his legs running, but maybe you can special exercise his problem leg so it doesn't stiffen up after a run. Otherwise, you're being as good a vet as I am."

"How should I exercise the leg?"

"Bathe it in cool water before you put the dressings on, then move it back and forth for about five minutes. Augie's strong enough to nurse as long as Grace will let him, but I don't want him running with other horses. You can put the adult horses in the corral next to him so he can get used to being around them, but keep him separate from them."

"So, are we out of the woods, Doc?" Marty Grimaldi asked.

"Not by a long shot. The foal's fine now, but you have to realize the rest of his body will grow much faster than his legs. As a colt, he'll weigh close to six hundred pounds on legs that won't be much bigger than they are now. Heck, the year after that he could be over a thousand pounds. By the time he's a full-blown stallion at four years he'll be sixteen or so hands high and weigh close to twelve hundred pounds. You know what I mean by 'hands high,' don't you Molly?"

"Yeah, I think so. The width of your hand is about four inches or so and you measure from the ground up to the back."

"The withers, yes," Doc said. "So, do you know how tall that would be if Augie is seventeen hands high?"

"About five feet tall?"

"Yes, and that doesn't count neck and head. Augie is going to be a very big boy and with you feeding him, he'll be huge. My point is that his legs will always be a worry. He runs too fast or over rough country and he could crumble. Don't get me wrong. A good breed stallion can pay off good for your daddy. He has an excellent bloodline and any horses he helps produce could become race horses."

"But not him?"

"I really don't recommend it, but I won't say for sure until he's a year old. He shouldn't be ridden until then anyway. We'll have plenty of time to nurse and evaluate that leg. Already he's done more than I thought he would. That's in large part because of you, but he's got the eyes, you know?"

"No, you lost me. What do his eyes have to do with whether he can run or not?"

"Aw, when I was watching him run he's got the eyes I always look for in a champion. His eyes get bigger when he runs. He's got focus and he runs for the joy of it. With you helping, he'll strengthen that old bone every day. He'll work at it. He'll test it. I was watching him licking at the dressings. He knows there's something there. He'll work until he drops. That foal wants to be fast and that's another of the reasons I don't want him running with other horses for a very long time. I saw those eyes. He won't want anyone faster than he is and he'll break his heart, or that leg, making sure no one gets in front of him for long."

"So, there's a chance?"

"Here's what I want you to believe so I don't confuse you. This horse shouldn't run competitively—ever. He has the heart of a champion and he'll risk it all to be the best. That will always be a danger for him and anyone on his back. That's what I say."

"Yeah, but you said it could be different after a year."

"Okay, let me say it another way. After a year we'll take another look. I just don't want you to get your hopes up. Because of you, this horse has value and we shouldn't try to turn him in to something he shouldn't be. Understand?"

"I think so, but it's okay for him to run on his own now?"

"It won't hurt him. The leg is good as long as he doesn't support weight and he isn't allowed to run free or run long periods of time. What would happen to you if you tried to run hard for two miles?"

"Well, my legs would sure get tired."

"Exactly. Your legs would be tired and not as strong as when you first started running. That's called muscle fatigue—tired muscles. When your muscles are tired you're more likely to fall or crumble—no different for a horse."

"I understand. When can he run with any other horses?"

"Wait a month and let him in with Amazing Grace. She'll watch over him. If he runs too much she'll stop him. She'll set the pace. Any questions, Marty?"

"No, Augie, you've been very clear. Hasn't Molly done a great job? I was ready to have him put down and maybe now he can help with breeding all over the county. Everyone knows he has Dancer's blood in his veins. Manny and I were saying the same thing about his eyes. He's a blazer, isn't he? I wish he could run because I'll bet he could be a dasher. You're right about the big picture. We'll be careful with him. When should Molly stop dressing the leg?"

"I'll come out again, but I think Molly can quit when school starts in the fall. Your little girl has saved a stallion for you, Martin. This horse will pay his way. Around that same time, you can start to corral him too, but I don't want him in the pasture. He gets to running out there and you'll never stop him."

As much as Molly loved Doc Cable, she didn't exactly listen to his advice. Doc said the left front leg should be exercised five minutes a day. Molly wrote in her notebook that she would double Doc's advice and exercise the leg ten minutes a day. Each morning she'd put a couple sugar cubes in her shirt pocket and the whole time Handsome Augie nuzzled to get at the cubes, Molly would lift the left leg up and down. After the first five minutes Molly would give up the first sugar cube and eventually the second, but not until the entire ten minutes was over and Augie had finished his extra exercise. Molly believed the left leg needed to be stronger than the others and the only way that could happen was for the left leg to work while the others rested. Molly began to double the calcium in Augie's feed. If calcium helped build stronger bones in people, why wouldn't it work with horses? She added vitamins to Augie's water and encouraged him to drink. Each night she'd record Augie's progress in her notebook.

It was the middle of August before Doc Cable returned and he was tremendously impressed with Handsome Augie's progress. Molly couldn't watch as her father and Manny secured Augie in crossties while the doctor tattooed numbers underneath the horse's upper lip. Doc confessed he hadn't done it earlier because he wasn't at all sure Augie would survive, but race horses must be tattooed in order to compete at any time in their lives. It was actually a compliment that Doc must beginning to have at least some faith that Augie might race someday, and now he was properly marked. Obviously, Handsome Augie didn't appreciate the compliment and Molly busied herself outside the barn until the entire ordeal was over.

"His mouth will be sore a few days," Doc said. "He might not take on much food and he may lose a few pounds in the next week or so. I wanted him to be healthy enough to take on the tattoo. I checked him from end to end, Molly. He's a fine horse."

"What about the leg?"

"Very strong and sturdy. You letting him run?"

"Only in the corral and only a half hour each day. He's so fast I can tell he's disappointed when I make him quit. He starts running and runs the whole time. He won't stop for sugar cubes any more. I had to go to carrots and apples. I slip the lead over his neck while he eats or he'll take off again."

"I know I said it before, but it's your dedication that gives this horse a chance. You're an amazing young woman, Molly. I want to talk to you about a couple things. Would that be okay?"

"You want to talk about Handsome Augie?"

"Aw, we already talked about him. He's in loving and caring hands. I don't worry about him with you on duty. I want to talk about you."

"Okay."

"You know how you can feel someone behind you? Sometimes you know when the phone will ring and who it will be. Other times you know something is going to happen and then it does? Everyone has that ability to one degree or another, but I can tell the future."

"Oh, Doc," Molly answered, "you mean about medical things?"

"No, I mean about people. Would you like me to tell your future right now? Okay, let me look at these magic leaves here on the lawn. See, they make a pattern and the way they're laid out I can tell exactly what's going to happen to a person."

"You can, huh?"

"Oh yeah," Doc said, running his fingers through white hair and pretending to study the leaves. "Aw, there you go. See the way that leaf is pointing toward the barn? That's the Handsome Augie leaf and he's going to be just fine and one day he'll chase the wind."

"You see that in a leaf?"

"Oh sure," Doc said. "See that one there—that really pretty one. That's the beauty leaf and it says you will be the most beautiful woman in the county and every boy will want to take Molly to the prom. Oops, look at the love leaf there. The love leaf says you will love, and be loved, better and stronger than anyone."

"Oh, Doc. You're so cute."

"You don't have to believe me, but you have to believe the leaves. See those yellow ones in kind of a pile? They tell me you can take on layers of problems and always find the right things to say and do. That one with the red tinges pointing up tells me you will always be very smart and successful and you'll always think things through completely before you act. Wow, look at that one. You'll be married before twenty-nine and have beautiful children—one with freckles and a smile as pretty as yours. I thought there was never anyone as pretty as your mom and now here you come. Yep, I've never read leaves as nice as yours. You sure are going to be someone special in this crazy world."

"That's what you wanted to tell me?"

"That's exactly what I wanted to tell you. You're very special and I'm honored to know you."

"You saw all that in the leaves?"

"Oh, yeah," Doc said. "The leaves never lie."

"I love you, Doc. You are the grandfather I never had. I want to be a legend like you are. Don't you know everyone loves you?"

"Right now I'm pleased that you do."

"That stuff about the leaves was just something you made up, huh?"

"Oh, no. Every bit of it is true."

"I so love you, Doc."

Doctor August Cable moaned his way to his feet and returned his ridiculous cowboy hat to the top of his head. He was bowlegged and he seemed more stooped over than Molly remembered. Maybe because Molly was getting taller Doc seemed shorter, but he was still a giant of a man. Today he'd come out to look at a horse and talk to a girl. Molly really didn't know if her father paid for these visits, but she never saw any money change hands. Molly would have loved to have seen Doc Cable back when he was a jockey. He still had the eyes of a champion. She held hands with Doc as they walked toward his Bronco and soon she watched his cowboy hat flopping up and down as he navigated the ruts in the road.

There was no doubt Molly Grimaldi had more hurts than the average twelve-year-old. Her mother's death not only left gigantic emotional holes, but also added chores no one else could do. After a month or two of her father's horrible cooking, Molly borrowed cookbooks from the library and slowly took over all the cooking right down to making grocery lists. She quietly took over the family garden, the housekeeping, the sewing, cleaning the stables, feeding the livestock, and now that Handsome Augie was an important part of her life, there didn't seem enough hours in the day. How would she manage when school started? Her father had talked about hiring someone to take care of the house, but Molly knew there wasn't enough money and she wouldn't let her father see how tired she was. On a farm, everyone pulls weight and complaining wastes precious time.

Marty Grimaldi rarely talked about the loss of his wife, but Molly never ventured out on the porch when she smelled pipe tobacco. A couple nights a week after chores were done and Manny went out to his cabin to sleep, Marty Grimaldi took his pipe out to the porch and he'd alternately stare at a curtain of stars and a rumpled picture he usually kept in his wallet. Molly knew the picture was the one of her mother in a wagon being pulled by Amazing Grace. There was a larger version of the same picture above the fireplace and she knew her dad needed his quiet time. Her dad didn't smoke his pipe too often, but when she smelled cherry scented smoke coming through the screen door she always stayed away. After about forty minutes, her father would come back in the house with red eyes. If Molly had learned not to complain, she had learned it from her father.

At the same time, Molly had more joy in her life than most girls her age. She had her father, Manny, the animals, and Doc. She had starry nights and had seen more sunrises and sunsets than any city girl. Her arms and legs were strong from hard work and every day she could snatch oranges from trees and catch fresh fish from a spring fed pond. Molly could watch an orange moon come over the orange grove not colored or sullied by city lights. She knew all about cooking and could ride a different horse every day. She had experienced life and death at close quarters and she totally understood the precious balance of nature. Sure, the girls in Ocala dressed better, had boyfriends, went to dances, and had over a hundred cable television stations, but those girls were going where pointed by others. Molly would be the architect of her own life and she would build a life of love, family, nature, friends, and, of course, Handsome Augie.

CHAPTER FOUR

A Death in the Family

Molly woke early the following Wednesday and there was commotion in the kitchen. There were voices beyond the usual chatter of Manuel and her father, and Molly put on a robe and brushed long hair to go out to see whom else was here and what was happening. There was something strange and hushed about these voices. It wasn't the usual bluster of ranchers talking about horses and farming. Something was going on and Molly rushed to the kitchen only to see Manny and her father seated at the kitchen table and the Kohler brothers and Mr. Davis leaning against the counter sipping coffee.

"What's up?" Molly asked, and it was only now she saw her father was crying. She hadn't actually seen her father crying in four years and now tears streamed wide paths down his cheeks. "Daddy, what's wrong?"

"Oh, Molly," her father said in a child's voice, "Augie's dead."

"My horse?"

"No, baby, Doc Cable."

"That can't be," Molly said. "He was just here last week."

"The boys came this morning to tell me. We think he had a heart attack and died in his sleep. He was a great man and he loved you so much."

"No!" Molly shouted and went to her room and slammed and locked the door. She didn't hear the last of what her father said and suddenly there was a tremendous buzzing in her ears and now she sat in the middle of the floor, her fingers interlaced around her knees and she began to howl. How could the unthinkable be true? How could Doc be dead? She rocked back and forth and years of tears streamed down her face. She cried loudly and shouted and ignored her father's knocks on the door. Doc was her very best friend and he had been part of her life as long as she could remember. He was always happy and funny and beautiful. Beyond her father, there was no other human being she loved so fiercely. When her mother died, Molly was barely nine years old and maybe she just didn't understand. She cried at the funeral, but somehow her mother's death didn't carry the sick knowledge she had now. She would never see Doc again. She would never hear him laugh and no one else said 'Aw' before starting a sentence—only Doc. No one told the future with leaves scattered on the ground—only Doc. No one else looked so silly and wonderful in a floppy cowboy hat. No one touched her cheek like Doc. No one walked like Doc. No one looked at a horse with Doc's eyes.

Now Molly understood death is absence. She moved from the floor to her bed and still Molly Grimaldi cried. This was the most terrible news of her life. This seemed so wrong. It should be that her mother's death would occupy such a position, but somehow this was worse and Molly struggled to understand. Perhaps because she was so young, maybe she didn't believe how final death is. She certainly knew now, and life without Doc was a horrible thought.

"Oh, Doc," Molly said aloud, "I'm so glad the last thing I said to you was how much I love you. I remember exactly what I said. I said, 'I so love you, Doc.' That's what I said and I always will. I hope you know everyone loved you. You were everything to us. It wasn't just our critters you took care of— you took care of us too, didn't you? I hope you were happy. I guess none of us checked on you and I'm sorry. I should have had you come out for dinner. I bet you ate late at night and all alone. I should have called you just to talk. You were my friend and now you're gone. I'm so sorry."

Molly wasn't sure what a pallbearer was, so when a tall thin woman approached her at the funeral home, Molly wasn't sure what the woman was saying. Immediately after she and her father and Manny entered Blalock's Funeral Home, the first thing they did was sign a book and then they went into the room where Doc's casket was surrounded by flowers. Molly walked awkwardly to the casket, knelt down next to her father, and she couldn't remember if she prayed or just stared. How could Doc be dead? Tears flowed widely down her face and she cried without sound. After a few moments her father rose to his feet and helped Molly away from the casket. That's when the woman approached.

"Karen," her father said as her embraced the woman Molly was sure she had never seen before. "You know how sorry I am. Your dad was my dad. Thank you for sharing him with us for so many years."

"I'm sorry I wasn't here with him," Karen said. "I called him from school nearly every day, but I wish I was here with him. He had all of you, but I know he was lonely after mom passed."

"What happened?" Marty asked.

"I got the call at six in the morning. His house was always such a mess I convinced him to hire Mrs. Carpenter to come in and clean a couple times a week. I actually hoped he and Mrs. Carpenter might hook up romantically, but she told me Dad never got the message. I doubt he ever considered anyone else after my mom. Anyway, she said Dad wasn't up with his coffee as usual and then she couldn't wake him. She called the doctor but Dad was gone. I think his heart failed for the very first time."

"I know what you mean," Marty Grimaldi answered. "Your father had more heart than anyone I have ever known. Do you remember this young lady?"

"I knew it was Molly the moment you two entered the room," the woman said. "Molly, you're beautiful. Dad said you are a future beauty queen."

"Hi," Molly said, "I'm so sorry about your dad. He was a grandfather for me. I guess I didn't know we met before."

"Yes, we did. I was home when your mom passed away, but I don't think we got to talk much. Heck, you were only a kid—not a woman like you are now. I know all about you."

"You do?"

"Oh, yes I do. I have been very jealous of you. With my dad, it was always. 'Molly-this or Molly-that.' Then when you named your horse after him I thought I'd never hear the end of it. He sure put a lot of stock in you, Molly Grimaldi. That's why I want to ask you a favor."

"A favor?"

"I'd like it very much if you would agree to be a pallbearer."

"I'm not sure what that is."

"Pallbearers help carry a casket. Usually men are pallbearers, but I think my father would want me to make an exception. Do you think you would do that?"

"I don't think I could."

"Honey, you don't do it by yourself, but I bet you would if you could. There are six pallbearers and I want you to be in the middle across from your dad. What do you think?"

"Aren't there more important people to do it?"

"No, you will be the most important of all the pallbearers because he loved you most. It is an honor you will always remember."

"I don't know how to thank you. What if I make a mistake?"

"A mistake would be not choosing you. I am the one to thank you."

"I don't even know what to call you. Should I call you Ms. Cable?"

"Only if I call you Ms. Grimaldi. How about we just go with 'Molly' and 'Karen'? My dad named me Karen because he liked the double 'K' sound—Karen Cable. Cable starts with a 'C' but sounds like a 'K'. Dad liked that."

"I like it too," Molly said and hugged a new friend.

In between listening to the adults, looking at an ashen colored Doc at the front of the room, and watching people wiping tears and sharing stories, Molly riveted her attention on Karen Cable. She looked close to thirty years old and she was absolutely beautiful. She was nearly six feet tall, thin, and her black hair was long and shiny. Even in a black dress, she looked like a model and she was warm and friendly and held hands with people as she spoke to them. She had seen pictures of Doc's daughter. As the preacher spoke from a podium, Molly glanced at her father. He was looking at Karen. Molly poked him in the ribs and he smiled.

Doctor August Winston Cable was laid to rest after a graveside ceremony in blistering sun. It seemed to Molly that everyone she had ever known was there. Later at the church, a microphone was passed around and people shared stories and thoughts about the passing of a wonderful man. Some of the stories were beautiful, about his devotion to animals, and others were funny, about his sense of humor.

When the microphone was passed to Molly, she said, "Doc was my best friend. He'll stay alive in my heart for as long as I live." She began to cry. Manny and her father hugged her as the minister retrieved the microphone and wished that all people had a friend like Doc Cable.

Then Karen Cable spoke.

"For my father, I thank all of you for coming. Today we bury my father, but memories of him will live on. My Dad made each one of us feel like we were the only person in his world. Even animals sensed his love, strength, and power. I remember when I was about eight-years-old; Dad let me go with him out to Mr. Gudding's farm. Mr. Gudding had a stallion that had been frightened by a thunder storm. No one could get near him. That horse had been out in the corral kicking and snorting for hours by the time Dad and I arrived. Dad grabbed an apple from the back seat of our car and walked right out into that corral. Mr. Gudding yelled for him to get out of there, but Dad stood in the middle of the corral with his arm outstretched with an apple in his palm. The stallion snorted and charged a few steps a couple times, but Dad stood there talking with that stupid apple in his hand. I was thinking that horse was surely going to mow down my father, he suddenly stopped snorting and stomping and inched closer to Dad. The whole time Dad was talking, 'Come here, little boy. You just got scared. Being scared is okay. Come on, now. The only cure for being scared is a little apple.' That giant stallion ate the apple from my father's hand. Dad slipped a lead around the big boy's neck and walked him back to his owner.

That's the day I decided I wanted to be a vet just like my dad. When I told him that, he looked at some leaves on the ground and read them like a fortuneteller. He said the leaves foretold that I was right; it would be a good idea. I knew that meant it was a good idea to my father and I went to veterinary school while learning compassion and understanding from him. Now, I would like to be your veterinarian to carry on for him."

While Karen spoke, Molly noted that her father did not take his eyes from the young woman. She felt a twinge that he would even look at a woman after her mother, but remembering his sadness, she realized that this new interest was good.

The barbecue after Doc's funeral seemed disrespectful to Molly. People talking and laughing and eating fried chicken just after burying a great man wasn't right. People should go home and be sad and quiet. It wasn't right that her own father should be sipping beer and talking and flirting with Karen. Molly felt she should go out behind the barn and wait until the party was over.

"I see you don't have a plate," Manny said. "You not hungry?"

"I just don't think we should be here."

"I respect that. You think we all should have gone home?"

"Yes, I do."

"That's one opinion, but I will give another opinion. At the church and cemetery we mourned the loss of our favorite man. We cried to have lost him from among ourselves. Now, as he would have us do, we celebrate his life. We share our sadness, but we also share our joy to have known such a man. Now we tell fun stories and are respectful to make sure we all remember Doc the same way. Now we share him in our hearts and hear more stories about him than we knew before. Now when we go home we remember to be thankful for his time with us, rather than sad. Does this make sense?"

"Yeah, I guess so."

"Prove it to me by getting some chicken and sharing a story or two. I think people would like to hear about Handsome Augie."

"Manny, I think I can eat something, but I don't have anything to say. I'd like to keep my feelings about Doc to myself a while longer. I sure didn't name my horse to prepare for this day. It's okay if I keep some things to myself, isn't it?"

"You bet it is, Molly. You grieve for Doc in your own way. If you believe a person is a unique collection of ideas and that Doc's personality and ideas live on, then he can never truly die."

"I believe that too, Manny. I believe Doc is alive inside my head. I can still see him in my mind. I just wish I could see him in front of me."

Molly cried again for Doc, and with Manny comforting her she began to regain control and dry her eyes. Manny walked Molly back to the barbecue. After a time she allowed herself a hamburger and beans and to laugh at the story about Doc her father was telling.

"So, I go out to the barn," her father said, "I can just feel this is going to be a weird day because on the way to the barn I see the crazy cat has climbed to the top of the barn and he's caught himself in the weathervane and he's meowing and kicking to beat the dickens. My wife had bought him a silly collar with rhinestones on it. The cat hated it. That collar got caught in the weathervane and each time the wind came up, the cat would twirl around until he could just get his stretched-out toes back on the roof. My wife sees this too and she's sure the cat is going to hang and still be stuck up on the weathervane. She gets hysterical and calls Doc. A little while later the three of us are standing getting drenched in a storm. It's raining cats and dogs and we see lightning in the distance. My wife starts screaming that 'Blinky' is going to get electrocuted and, all of a sudden, Doc is high-tailing it up a ladder. Doc and his big cowboy hat are up on the roof with the spiraling cat. The cat has never seen Doc before and, every time Doc gets close, it starts hissing. I guess Doc decided if he acted like a cat, maybe Blinky would like him and let him reach for the collar. Doc stars meowing like a cat and moving his hands like the paws of a cat. Now, I'm laughing so hard tears are streaming down my face along with the rain. The wind is whistling. Doc's hat is flopping, the cat is spinning and they are barely holding on, but Doc is still meowing. All of a sudden, the collar flips off the weathervane. The freed cat races around Doc, and down the ladder he runs. My wife snatches up the cat and now it starts meowing and doing the paw thing for Doc to come down. For a long time, I could not look at Doc without thinking about him up on the roof that day."

It was the last story of the day and the best one of all. Even though her dad was forty-two now, Molly couldn't help but notice how the women in the crowd seemed to be particularly interested in her father's story. Karen Cable seemed particularly interested, but her father was much too old for her. She couldn't even be thirty years old, but she sure was paying attention. Molly's dad was six feet tall and thin and strong from working the farm, but why would women be interested in him? He did have a full head of blonde hair that was always sun streaked and he was always bronze colored from working in the sun. He had high cheekbones and even Molly had to admit he had muscular arms and wonderfully veined and masculine hands. Even as he walked Karen to her father's Bronco, Molly couldn't quite figure the younger woman's attraction. He was just her dad and it was strange that women should find him attractive.

"So, Dad," Molly said as they left the Baxter farm and headed back out onto the blacktop. "You think Karen is pretty?"

"Yeah, Dad," Manny said from the back seat, "you think that Karen girl is pretty at all?"

"Oh, hush you two. You know she's beautiful."

"You gonna ask her to the dance?" Manny asked.

"Maybe you'll go steady," Molly offered.

"Oh boy, I can see this is going to be something. I just said she was pretty."

"Dad, I think you said she was 'boootiful'."

"Oh, don't start. She'll be a nice vet for the community and, okay, she's nice to look at."

"So you admit you were looking at her all day," Molly said. "You were like those surprised animals in cartoons with their eyes all bugged out."

"My eyes were not 'bugged out'."

"Boss," Manny said. "Your eyes were bugged out."

"Her eyes were pretty big, Dad."

"Molly, it was her father's funeral."

"I'm not saying she wasn't showing respect, but she sure was being nice to you. Her mind and heart were at the funeral, but her eyes were on you."

"She's too young for me."

"Better tell her that."

"Oh, stop it, you two. I doubt Karen would be interested in a farmer. She probably has a boyfriend or six from school. I'm not educated and I'm surely not rich."

"Karen is farm people too, Boss," Manny offered. "She went to school so she could work with farmers and ranchers. Her daddy wasn't rich. Heck, half the time people paid their vet bills in sides of beef or oranges. Yep, Molly, I think your daddy is about to need lots of visits from the new vet. Every time one of the horses sneezes or one of the chickens gets the hiccups, we may just have to call the new vet over to have a look."

"You two just won't let up. I'm not interested in anyone. I had my time in love and I just think I have enough to worry about without cluttering my mind with other things."

"I think you'll be able to move some clutter off to one side while you think about Karen," Molly said. "You're a rascal, Dad."

Later that night after dishes were cleared and the livestock fed and watered for the night, Marty Grimaldi was out on the porch and cherry flavored tobacco smoke worked its way into the house. This time Molly went out to be with her father and this time his eyes weren't red. They sat the longest time without speaking and finally her father asked, "You really think she was looking at me?"

"No doubt about it," Molly answered. "She was looking at you all day long."

"Is that something that's okay with you?"

"I'm not sure yet. At first I was thinking it was a wrong thing for you two to be interested in each other, but when I tried to figure out why that was true I couldn't think of any reasons. I don't know how I feel. Do you know how you feel?"

"No, I don't guess I do. It's something to think about."

"While you're thinking, someone else will be moving in on her. I just know one thing for sure."

"What's that?"

"That Doc would approve. You being with Karen would make him smile."

"You think so?"

"Yep. Now I'm going to say goodnight to my horse."

Molly strolled to the barn and all the way she smiled that her father was like an eighth grader interested in the new girl at school. To be sure, no one could ever replace her mother but Karen wouldn't ever try to do such a thing. Additionally, her father knew nothing but hard work with little return. Maybe he needed to think about something, someone, new. All the while Molly brushed Handsome Augie she thought about how quickly lives could change.

"Look at you, Handsome. You're growing every day. Tomorrow I'll let you run. You'll like that, huh? You won't even look the same in a year. I guess I won't either. I hope we're both going to be okay. Our friend got buried today. We'll miss Augie, won't we? He took good care of both of us. Maybe someday you'll be a champion and somehow Doc will know. I don't know what's in store for us. My life has changed so much and your life is just getting started. Let's just agree now to spend our lives together."

Handsome Augie liked it when Molly talked to him. Her voice was soft and soothing and she always ended a conversation with an apple. While Manny and Mr. Grimaldi fed and worked him, Augie knew he belonged only to Molly. When Molly was in the corral, Augie would follow her like a big dog and listen to her commands.

Doc taught her to always keep commands to one word or a short phrase and always say a name before the command. 'Augie: Come!' 'Augie: Whoa.' They were simple commands and more would be added, but Augie needed to know who was boss and Molly was boss. Doc had explained that horses often test owners to see if they were amateurs. Doc said training should start immediately and even a foal should know who is boss. Meek owners wait too long and end up with a stubborn horse resistant to training. It was good for Augie to focus and pay attention and Molly would be sure he did.

Molly wanted to remember everything Doc had told her, because now his voice had been silenced. Quiet tears filled Molly's eyes as she made Augie's concoction of oats, calcium, vitamins, chopped carrots and apples. It was a soggy mess that her horse loved and each day Molly noted the weight and mixture she made in her journal. She measured each ingredient as a scientist would and increased amounts each Wednesday. Handsome Augie was thriving and getting healthier each day. The last time Doc saw Augie he said he had never seen a foal so shiny and bright-eyed. While there still was concern about Augie's leg, there was no concern about his overall health. Doc said so and Doc was never wrong.

CHAPTER FIVE

Runway Models and Country Girls

While Molly reluctantly wore a dress for Doc's funeral, wearing a dress to school were out of the question. Her father took her into Ocala to buy a few new outfits for school, but each time her father held up a dress or something frilly, Molly would roll her eyes. By the end of the morning, Molly agreed to new tennis shoes, three blouses, and two pair of new jeans. She had one pair of dress slacks at home, and the flat black pumps she had worn to the funeral. They were enough if she had to dress up for an occasion. Skirts, high heels and makeup was for city girls. Molly had no interest in them.

"Maybe," her father suggested, "you might want to buy some lipstick."

"What for?"

"You're going to be a teenager in a couple months and I just thought you might want to get some lipstick just in case you go to a dance or something."

"You don't need lipstick to go to a dance."

"I just thought you might want to have some handy in case you need it."

"Why would I need it?"

"Don't get testy about it. I'm just alerting you that as a dad I don't know the kinds of things you might want to buy. Your mom could have helped us with this, but I just don't know. You have to tell me the woman stuff you need."

"Dad, I'll tell you when I need important things and I can get most of what I need when you take me shopping for groceries. They have lipstick and stuff at the same store. Is that okay?"

"Yeah, sure. I feel somewhat a failure when it comes to stuff like this. I'm sorry."

"Oh, hold on my dad and best friend. I won't hear that from you. You treat me just fine. My life is good and I couldn't be more pleased to be your daughter. How's that?"

"That's very nice, Molly. I think everyone needs to know they're okay with the people they love, and it's nice that I'm for sure okay with you. You're pretty okay with me, too."

"Well, thank you, Father."

"You know what I mean. You cook and clean and take care of all kinds of things around the farm. Don't think I don't appreciate all the things you do. Now you've taken on that horse and I worry you're overworked."

"I'll let you know if I feel that I am."

"No, you won't. Sometimes you are so tired that you fall asleep in seconds. When I come in to check on you, you're so cute, I stay a minute or so. Your little nose twitches while you sleep."

"You watch me sleep?"

"For a little while every night. You are the most precious thing in my life. You won't be a little girl much longer and pretty soon you'll be married and off with your own family."

"Yep, I'm getting married next week. What *are* you talking about?"

"Just that years fly by very quickly. Molly, why are we talking about this in the middle of the store?"

"Because all of a sudden you want to buy me some lipstick."

"Do you want some lipstick?"

"No! Will you stop it?"

"You don't want to look like the other girls?"

"I don't have any need to look like the other girls. Is it okay if I just look and act like Molly?"

"Works for me."

"Then let's get out of here. I know women are supposed to love shopping and malls. I'd just rather get home and see how Augie is doing."

"Are we saying we like animals more than people?"

"Dad, I like lots of people and even some of the people at school, but, yeah, I might like animals better. They just seem more honest, you know? When Augie sees me in the morning I can tell he's really happy to see me. People just tell you they're happy to see you, but I'm not sure if they really are. People make up moods for attention. Animals have moods too, but all of theirs are real."

Perhaps the most difficult thing about the first day of school was leaving her father, Manny, and her wonderful friend Augie. From his first day on the planet, Augie had never spent an entire day without Molly. Even when she came out to clean the barn and tack room, she'd let Augie out of his stall and he would follow her around like a giant puppy. If she watered down the concrete walkway, Augie would sniff her hair and try to bite her ponytail. Each time she used the pitchfork to put fresh hay in the stalls, Augie would nudge her backside and sometimes push her down. He would get in her way and try to take attention away from her chores, and, sooner or later, Molly would stop long enough to brush him or produce a carrot or apple from a secret hiding place. Augie's tactic worked every time and, too often, Molly would spend time with Augie rather than keep up with her chores. Augie had learned to disappear back into his stall and return with his currybrush tucked in the corner of his mouth. His trick was so cute that Molly never resisted brushing him for fifteen minutes, and she would swear Augie would smile the entire time. He was a wonderful horse and Molly always talked to him as she brushed.

"You love this, don't you Augie?" Molly would ask as she brushed his jet-black mane. "You love every minute. I'm pretty sure you're getting very spoiled, but I'm not sure it's a bad thing. We all like to feel a little spoiled, don't we? School starts soon and you'll need to understand I won't see you as much. I promise you an apple each day and I'll put you in the little corral each morning it isn't raining. Fair deal? You can work on your running and get that leg nice and strong. You'll be brushed every day at four and then I promise to have our little talk before I go to bed. I'll come out to sleep here either Friday or Saturday nights and that's how we'll do things for a while. Augie, you following all this?"

Augie was just listening to the voice he loved and enjoying the brushing. The words made no sense to him at all. The words did not matter. Molly and Augie were each other's very best friend in the world.

CHAPTER SIX

A Visit to Another Century

The first day of school started with disaster. Molly was ready and waiting for the big day, dressed in her new jeans and one of the new blouses, but there was huge trouble waiting at the end of the driveway, where three county trucks were parked. Manny wouldn't tell her what was going on, and her father was down at the end of the rutted drive flailing his arms while talking to a county worker. He was angry. Molly watched through the window as her father was stomping and pointing and the man he spoke to tried to hand him a white paper. Her father finally snatched the paper from the man's hand, and in a second it was on the ground. Then her father was stomping on it with his boots. The trucks took off across the pasture, crossing Grimaldi land, and Marty Grimaldi was charging back to the house with fire in his eyes.

"What's going on, Manny?" Molly asked as Manny sipped coffee. "Who are these people and why is Daddy so mad?"

"You'll find out soon enough. You'd be better to go out to the bus out the back door and talk to him when you get back from school."

"No way am I doing that," Molly said firmly. "This is my farm too. What is going on, Manny?"

"I don't think you should talk to your father just now. Please, just go to school."

But Molly asked the moment her father entered the doorway, "Dad, what's happening?"

"Please, just go to school. I'll tell you about it later."

"Tell me now."

"You know what?" Marty Grimaldi shouted, "I give you a lot of room for a little girl. You give me some room as a man. I'm saying don't badger me now. Go to school like I just told you. For once, do what I say!"

"I was only asking."

"And I'm telling you to go to school!"

Molly burst into tears and ran around her father and out the door. Behind her she could hear her father shouting like he never had before and now she could hear dishes breaking and she heard words she had never heard her father say before. Crying and nearly at the end of the driveway, Molly could still hear her father shouting. Normally Marty Grimaldi was the most gentle man in the world, but not this day. Down the road, Molly could see the flashing lights of the school bus. She struggled to stop her tears before the bus got close. It was hopeless. She was sobbing. All the other students would see her crying like a kindergartner on the first day of school. Molly turned toward the house and wondered whether she should tell the driver she was sick and run back home. At the same time she could see her father's jeep racing toward her at breakneck speed. Her father was driving, and he was still shouting.

"Molly! Don't get on that bus! Don't get on that bus!"

Her father hit the brakes, nearly slamming the jeep into one of the posts announcing 'Three-M Farm and Ranch.' Quickly he threw the jeep into reverse aiming it at the house. In an instant his long legs flipped out of the jeep and he was next to Molly.

"Get in the jeep. Face the house," he said firmly. "I'll talk to the driver. Do what I say. Do it."

"Dad..."

"Do it now!"

In seconds the bus arrived and yellow doors opened. Marty Grimaldi walked to the bus to talk to driver Gina Williams.

"Hey, Gina," he said in a surprisingly calm voice compared to the wild man he was seconds ago. "Another school year, huh? I bet the kids are all excited."

"Yeah sure," Gina said. "Something wrong?"

"Naw, but I have to bring Molly in a little late. I need her at the house for an hour or so. Would you tell them at the office I'll bring her by in an hour or so?"

"Sure. Is everything okay?"

"Oh yeah, everything's fine. I just need an extra pair of hands for a while. She'll be in directly."

If nothing else, Molly was thrilled the bus was gone and she didn't turn when several students shouted her name. Suddenly she began to cry uncontrollably. Her father approached on the passenger side of the jeep. He moved to hug her and Molly pushed him away. She put her face in her hands and cried and shook.

"Molly? Molly?"

"What?"

"I couldn't let you go to school like this."

"You ordered me to go."

"I know and I'm sorry."

"You talk to me like garbage and now you're sorry?"

"I've never been this sorry in my life. Please look at me. Please listen. You don't have to forgive, but please listen to me."

"What about the trucks?" Molly asked. "Tell me why the trucks made you like this."

"I don't care about the trucks right now. I care about you. You are the only person in the world I treasure. No one else. I will never ever hurt you again like I did today. I love you beyond all others. I was mad at the guys in the trucks and took out my anger on you. I am so sorry."

"Dad, it will be okay," Molly said, trying to stop crying.

"Oh, no, my losing control is never okay. You'll get your share of tears, but none should be caused by me. Just tell me you accept my apology."

"Stop it, Dad. I'm okay now. Am I going back to school?"

"Soon enough, but you haven't answered my question."

"I know you're sorry, and I accept that you didn't mean to snap at me. I am hurt by the way you did what you did. I stiill don't know why the guys in the trucks made you so angry."

"That's part of why I came to get you. I couldn't let you go to school in the condition I created. Maybe if you see what made me so angry, you'll understand."

"Just tell me."

"Nope," Marty Grimaldi said, jumping back into the jeep. "You have to see it to understand."

"But if you go back by the truck guys, aren't you going to get angry again?

"I'll show my anger in court, but never again in front of you."

"Court?"

"Let's go for a ride," Marty said. He put the jeep in gear and plopped over the ruts, onto the lawn, around the barn and back toward the orange groves. It wasn't long before Molly saw the three county trucks and heard noises above the roar of the jeep's engine.

"What's that noise?"

"Chainsaws, Molly," her father answered. "That musical sound you hear is chainsaws."

"What are the men doing?"

"Well, Molly of mine," her father said, shutting off the jeep a hundred or so feet from the grove. "Have you ever heard of canker?"

"Like the sores you get in your mouth?"

"Well, kind of, but the canker we're talking about here is called 'citrus canker'."

"What's that?"

"According to the Department of Agriculture, half of Florida's orange trees have citrus canker, a disease that fruit trees get that spreads from tree to tree and can infect entire groves."

"So, what happens?"

"So, they cut down your trees."

"They're cutting down all of our trees?"

"No, we get to keep the southern section, and half of the west. We're going to lose three hundred trees."

"Do we get paid for them?"

"We get seedlings."

"Seedlings?"

"They replant two seedlings for every tree they take down. In six years, we'll have twice as many trees."

"But what happens until then?"

"We try to make it. We'll lose a third of our crop. They came through a month or two ago and marked a bunch of trees. We thought they were marking the trees for research, but suddenly they send a crew to cut them down. We're actually fortunate. Had the trees all been planted in one place, we'd have lost all of them."

"What do you mean?"

"The groves have to be one thousand or more feet apart or else they just keep cutting. The other two groves are two thousand feet apart. My father must have known what he was doing."

"I don't understand."

"My father planted every one of these trees on his hands and knees. I helped him and he purposely planted three groves. I thought it was stupid at the time because we'd have to drive all over the farm at harvest time. Back then he said he was doing it because storms might ruin all the trees if he kept them together. He also said he wanted to make sure he was never wiped out by pesticides or germs. He couldn't have known about canker, but your grandfather was a very smart man."

"I still don't get what canker is."

"It's a virus. It doesn't destroy the fruit, but it ruins their outside appearance and the oranges can't go to market because the virus can be spread. Manny showed me a bushel of oranges a few weeks ago, and they definitely had the canker. There is no cure. I guess I knew this day would come."

"They're going to cut down the trees?"

"Every single one in this grove. If you count the ones Manny and planted last fall, that's almost four hundred."

"We'll lose all that money?"

"Yes, my Molly," her father answered. "For six years, we'll lose one third of the orange crop. That's a big hit for 3-M. We'll make it through. We always have."

"Now I understand why you were so mad."

"I still should never have been mad at you. I wanted to save the oranges we could that were not affected. Most of the trees in that grove are still fine, but there's no time now. We lose all of them."

Now father and daughter watched as a crew of men with chainsaws cut down their orange trees. Five more men jockeyed tree after tree into a huge grinding machine that sprayed wood pulp and juice into a huge dump truck. Once Molly looked toward her father. Tears trailed down his cheeks and he didn't bother to wipe them. "My father planted these trees," he said.

Before eleven o'clock the trees were gone in the huge dump truck. A giant grinding machine ground stumps even with the soil and another truck drove a straight line while men planted seedlings, two for every tree that had been destroyed. The planting was of little comfort to Marty Grimaldi. Molly would be an adult before these new trees would bring any profit to 3-M Ranch and Farm. After watching a while, he slid down into the driver's seat and started the jeep's engine.

"Let's get you to school."

"You think I should bother to go?"

"Yeah, I do. At least you can settle in, see your friends, and get your schedule."

"But I'll feel silly walking in at lunch time."

"But you'll worry about tomorrow all night tonight if you don't go. I couldn't let you go this morning."

"I'm okay now, Dad," Molly said. "But is the ranch going to be okay? This is really going to hurt us, isn't it?"

"You know how small the profit margin is. We still have the rest of the harvest and Manny's tomato crop will help. We'll make it through the winter, but come spring we might need to sell the ten acres near the highway."

"No!" Molly answered.

"No, what?"

"This is 3-M Farm," Molly answered. "The three Ms stand for 'Marty-Molly-Manny'. I know two of those 'M's are going to vote 'no'. Manny won't want to sell and neither will I. You know they'll just build houses there. Do you really want a subdivision on Grimaldi land?"

"Of course I don't, but you have to know almost all the farms are gone and this morning you learned a little of why that is. Either being taxed to death or squeezed out by development, sooner or later you know this farm won't be allowed to exist."

"Oh no," Molly said firmly. "We cannot let them get the farm or even chew it off a bite at a time. This farm belonged to your father and his father. I want this farm to belong to me. I know you gave Manny a piece of ownership, but even he knows the farm is mostly ours. We have to find a way to keep the entire farm. I don't care if we have to charge schools to bring out little kids to see a working farm or raise bees to make honey, but we can't sell one inch of land."

"These your final words on the subject?"

"Dad, you know I'm right. I don't think I want to live on a lot with nosy neighbors left and right. I can just see you planting petunias in little pots to hang from a concrete porch. Then maybe we could walk the sidewalk and greet the Baxters and the Brewsters, and dodge little bratty kids on skateboards and bicycles."

"I get your point."

"I'm not sure you do. Do you really want your father's farm to be streets and sidewalks and basketball courts? I know I don't. We're ranchers and ranchers and land are as connected as the moon and stars. I know the world is becoming a smaller place. I've seen that in my lifetime. Your grandfather would have shot the people on our land today."

"You think I should have shot the county workers?"

"I'm just saying your grandfather would have shot them. We have to follow rules and I guess we have to do our part to stop the canker thing. I'm just saying that no one ever tears down a subdivision to build a farm. We have to hold the land."

"How old are you?" her father asked, smiling. "You go to school and learn to be smart enough to hold the farm, no matter what. We don't have college in our family and you'll be the first Grimaldi to get a degree. I'll hold the farm for you until you're ready to take over."

"Thank you for showing me why you were so mad. I understand now. Until you marry Karen, I'm all you have."

"Who said I'm marrying Karen?"

"Can't talk now, Dad. I have to go to school."

"I love you, Molly."

"And I love you. Please never again do what you did this morning. We need each other."

"I'll try never to have to apologize to you again."

Marty Grimaldi knew the subject would never be brought up again. Molly Grimaldi was that special kind of person who visits a subject only once and, once thoroughly discussed, the subject is never brought up again. It was this way even with the death of her mother. Breast cancer and its treatments were discussed in detail, and when her mother died, Molly knew what had happened and never visited the subject after the funeral. Her grandmother told her bad things can happen to good people and she remembered. Even though Marty knew she discussed the subject with her horse, even Doc's death was not a subject for dinner discussion. The closest she had come to even addressing Doc's death was this quick mention that her father might marry Karen. Molly Grimaldi was very special and, even with the face of losing his cherished orange trees, Marty Grimaldi managed a smile.

Molly explained her tardiness to school to a stout woman in the main office and soon she was escorted to the counseling center to pick up her schedule. Thankfully, Mr. Owen was her counselor. He decided there was no need for her to enter class already in session. It would have been embarrassing for her to walk in late and be the center of attention on her first day in a new school. Mr. Owen handed her a map of the building and walked with her to the counseling office door.

"Tell you what you do instead of going to class," Mr. Owen said. "Go find your locker, get that baby opened and closed a few times, and then backtrack trough the classrooms you missed so you'll know where they are tomorrow. By the time you get done with all that it'll be time for fifth hour and you can walk in right on time."

"Sounds great to me," Molly said. "Nice to meet you, Mr. Owen."

"Nice to meet you, Ms. Grimaldi. You stop in to see me any time."

Kennedy Junior High was less than two years old and was a beautiful building. Molly walked the halls, and found the rooms for English, math and music. She and her father had seen the building during orientation, and Molly now reluctantly admitted to herself it never would have been built without the need created by so many new families moving to the Ocala area. The gymnasium was spectacular. Every classroom was bright and cheerful and the library was filled with computers. Molly never had the heart to ask her father for a computer. He didn't seem to know how essential computers were for a kid's education. She hoped she could use these computers and save to buy one of her own.

In fifth hour English, Molly exchanged superficial hugs with Mary Ann Buffa and Darlene Klebba. They were her friends in sixth grade. Both wore designer outfits and several of the other girls in class were dressed like they were going to a dance. Molly was surprised how much makeup they used. Molly didn't even own a purse, although several of the girls did and produced mirrors and lipstick just before the bell rang to start class. Molly watched and smiled as two girls put on too much lipstick. Girls like Mary Ann and Darlene were in the majority now, and it was fine they lived their lives however they chose. It was strange, though, how people from two different worlds sat next to one another in the same classroom. Molly felt she belonged to a different century. If wearing lipstick and striking poses was new world, Molly was content to live at 3-M Ranch.

Molly was an excellent student and hadn't missed a day of school since taking three off for her mother's funeral. Even though it was nice to be with people her own age and some of her teachers were smart and funny, school was an interruption of the farm life she loved and preferred. She'd rather be home with her father, Manny, and, especially, Handsome Augie. But vocal music class was special. Molly had a beautiful voice and liked performing in talent shows, and one of the boys in class was very cute.

The dead giveaway was that he was new in town and new to the school was that his skin was snow white. Almost all the kids who lived in Ocala were tanned by Ocala's summer sun. The kids from the subdivisions had swimming suit tans. Molly had what her friends called a 'farmers' tan,' face and legs tan while arms above her sleeves were white. Molly had never been a sun worshipper because she was sure the sun produced even more freckles. The new kid sure was handsome and he carried himself well. Molly judged he had confidence because he signed up for vocal music with a bunch of seventh grade girls. His name was Daniel. He immediately told the teacher and the class, "call me 'Danny' or 'Dan' and forget you ever heard the name 'Daniel.' For this, I thank you all very much." It was kind of cool that he spoke easily in front of strangers. Several of the prettier girls giggled and stared at him. Danny followed Molly to her locker and got on the same bus. Danny waved to her and motioned to a front seat he had saved.

"Could you sit with me, or else no one will sit with the new kid?" Danny said.

"Sure, I guess," Molly answered and immediately discovered the new kid had great blue eyes and perfect teeth. "I was going to sit in back, but this is good."

"Did I get that your name is Polly?"

"No, Polly is a parrot. I'm Molly."

"Even better," Danny said. "I'm Dan Freeman—nice to meet you, Molly. What's your last name?"

"Grimaldi."

"Molly Grimaldi," Dan said, listening to the name. "I thought I was going to meet you this morning."

"Really?"

"Yeah, I saw you waiting by the bus stop, but you didn't get on the bus. You live on a farm, huh?"

"All my life. How could you see me? I think I had my back turned."

"Your hair. No one at the school has hair like yours."

"Is that good?"

"Oh, yeah—really good. So, do you like living on a farm?"

"I don't know anything else, but I don't think I'd like anything else."

"I'm jealous."

"Do you live in one of the new subs?"

"Yeah, my dad got transferred down here in July. I couldn't believe it—one day I'm playing baseball in Baltimore and the next day we're packing for Florida."

"You think you'll like it?"

"My friends were all jealous that I was moving close to Disney World and that I won't have to deal with ice and snow any more. I think I'm going to hate it. I've met exactly four people so far. I'm counting you if that's okay."

"So, you have a big new house?'

"It's brand new, but all of them are. I'd rather live on a farm. Do you have an old farmhouse and everything?"

"Yeah, my grandfather was born in our house and now my dad owns it."

"I think that's cool. What does '3-M' mean? Isn't that scotch tape? I thought that's what the sign said across the road to your farm."

"You catch everything, Dan Freeman. The three 'M's stand for Marty, Molly, and Manuel. Marty is my dad and Manuel has worked with us over twenty years, so my dad gave him fifteen per cent of the farm."

"I've been on a farm twice in my life—once on a field trip and the other time on a hay ride. What all do you have on your farm?"

"Well, we raise oranges and vegetables on part of it. Then we have chickens, thirty or so cows, and seventeen horses. Ah, what else? We have a twenty year old dog named 'Scooter' who mostly just stays on the porch. We have a few barn cats, but only one of them will let you touch him. We feed them, but they're 'drop-offs' from city people who didn't want them around so they live around the barn and we think they keep down the mice. That's about it—pretty boring, huh?"

"Are you kidding? It sounds great. If we get to be friends, could I see your farm some day?"

"Sure, I guess so, but right now all my time's taken up with a foal right now. I'm not saying that to brush you off. I'm saying that because it's true."

"Did you say, 'a fold'?"

"No, I said a foal. A foal is what you call a horse when it's first born."

"I thought a new born horse was a colt."

"Actually, a horse isn't officially a colt for a year or more. It doesn't matter. A horse is a horse. Anyway, this foal is only three months old and he had a broken leg when he was born, so I've been nursing him along."

"That is so cool. So, Molly with the hair and the freckles also raises horses?"

"Well, Manny and I and my father do. Augie is really my project, but we all help with all the horses."

"Augie? Who is Augie?"

"Oh, Augie is my horse. I named him after the vet who took care of him, but that's a long story. Anyway, let me answer your question. You can come to visit the farm in a month or so if you still want to. We have some other problems with the orange groves and, with Augie and all that, I'll barely have time for school."

"So you have lots of chores, huh? My sister and I fight about who takes out the garbage."

"There's lot of chores on a farm, Danny, and none of them can wait. Horses and cows are hungry today and can't wait for tomorrow. When it storms, city people go inside. That's when we have to go outside to make sure the livestock and crops are secure. Anything else you want to know?"

"I'm just happy you'll let me come out to see the place. Anything you want to know?"

"Okay, why does Danny from Baltimore take vocal music class?"

"Partly because I registered late and there weren't many electives left to choose from, but I had a little band in Baltimore."

"You did? Were you any good?"

"We were terrible. I didn't realize how bad we were until I listened to one of our tapes. We were loud, but we were terrible. I was lead singer and I have to admit moving was a nice way to break up the band without hurting anyone's feelings."

"You still have any of the tapes?"

"I threw all of mine out with the trash, but I'm afraid my friends and some girls still have copies. I do like to sing and I don't worry much about what people say."

"Me either. So, how was it moving out of Baltimore?"

"It wasn't as terrible as it sounds. We were only there for two years. Before that, we lived in Boston, before that outside of Detroit. My dad is a computer guy who creates software for companies, so we live close to where he works. He got a big contract working with a hotel chain down here, but, in a couple years, we'll be gone again. Just as I start to like a place, we move again."

"It's kind of an adventure, right? You get to see all the different parts of the country."

"I'd trade with you today. You might think your family living on the same farm isn't a big deal, but I think I'd love that."

"I do love it, Danny. I get teased at school and sometimes I'm jealous of kids with no chores and lots of luxuries, but I like my life. Grimaldis have been ranchers for generations and I won't change that."

"Don't the developers try to buy your farm?"

"All the time. My dad has meetings all the time, but he would never sell."

"What if they offered a million dollars?"

"I don't know how much they offer, but my dad says sometimes it's hard to turn them down. He says he'd never have to work again, but I think that's the part that scares him. My dad wouldn't know what to do without working the farm. My stop is the next one. It's been nice talking to you."

"Molly with the hair and the freckles, it's nice talking to you."

"You making fun of my freckles?"

"I love them and want to count every one."

"Bye, Danny," Molly said and jumped the three steps off the bus. She walked under the 3-M sign and turned around. Danny was still looking at her.

CHAPTER SEVEN

A Sad Day for 3-M Farm

Molly threw down her books, changed into Levis and a checkered shirt, and made a sandwich. She ate quickly and grabbed two apples from the bowl, then headed out to the barn to see Augie. Her father and Manny were nowhere around and Molly figured they must be out in the grove. Molly was deep in thought about school, butchered orange trees, and a boy named Danny. She hardly noticed Augie was out in the corral. Augie had seen her and he whinnied and pawed until he got her attention.

"Handsome Augie!" Molly shouted, joining her horse at the rail of the corral. "Where have you been all day? I missed you."

Augie was very excited. He had never been without Molly for this many daylight hours and he nuzzled at her face and neck as if he had found a lost friend. Soon enough Augie used twitching lips to move down Molly's arm to her hand where she hid the first apple. Augie knew Molly never came empty handed and Molly offered the apple and watched Augie chomp the apple until the juice ran down the corners of his mouth. Immediately, he seemed to sense there was a second apple and he sniffed and snorted until Molly backed up and showed him the second apple.

"Now, you watch," Molly said to Augie. She heaved the apple halfway across the corral. Augie didn't quite follow the flight of the apple and first he checked Molly's hands. This must have been very confusing to him. Augie turned around and then turned back to Molly. She held in her laughter. Her horse scanned the corral. Suddenly he saw the apple and looked at Molly. "Well, go get it."

Like a giant dog playing a game of fetch, Augie bounded toward the apple. In just a few long strides he reached the apple, and chomped it with satisfaction. Then, as if he had won a game, he ran around the corral and zoomed past Molly at a dead run. This is what the game had been about in the first place. Molly wanted to see what would happen if Augie broke into an abrupt run and what his legs would do if he had to bend all the way to the ground. She watched the front legs as Augie ran and he ran without hesitation or pain. She watched his flanks bob with each stride and his gait was even and smooth. Soon Augie ran back to Molly. She felt his chest and he was barely winded. She climbed to the top of the split rail fence and talked to her horse as she had every day of his life.

"Handsome, handsome, handsome," Molly said, and she traced her finger around the near perfect white star centered between Augie's eyes. "You just might be the most handsome horse there ever was in the history of horses. It's true, Augie. When the fillies see you, you'll be busy at your first dance. I was watching you run. You think maybe someday you'd like to be a racehorse? I've been working on an idea we'll talk about soon. You think maybe you'd like to get out in the pasture and run with no fences in the way? I have to talk to Karen about your leg and then maybe that's what I'll have you do. You just keep getting stronger and then we'll see what we want to do about you. Maybe for your Christmas present I'll open the pasture gate and let you fly. You have no idea what I'm saying, do you? All you know for sure is Molly's out of apples. It's a shame I can't feed you oranges. We have plenty of those—or at least we used to. Now, let's get this rope on and get you fed and brushed."

Molly used a strong stroke with a currycomb and Augie's skin seemed to quiver and vibrate behind each stroke. He was a beautiful animal and had the makings of a majestic stallion. Already he was strong and he held his head high like an aristocrat. He was jet-black and the color was vibrant and even from his ears to his tail. He had the pride and power of a thoroughbred mixed in with an arrogance that said he knew he was handsome and that other horses one day would be forced to give him room and respect. At present, all horses on the Grimaldi farm gave respect to Dashaway Dancer. He was the dominant horse. When Manny filled the hay bins out in the pasture, all other horses waited for the Dancer to eat first. When fresh water was added to the half barrels in the corral, Dancer drank and all others waited. Someday it would be this way for Handsome Augie.

Molly used the crossties in Augie's stall to hold him still while she exercised his front legs. Already his legs had grown heavier and stronger and now it was harder to lift and bend them at the knee. Doc Cable would be very proud of the foal he helped save. Augie was extremely strong and healthy and Molly was pleased at how well he could run. After school tomorrow she'd bring apples and carrots and throw them one at a time. It was good for Augie to run short sprints and then have to bend.

"Hey, Augie," Molly said, untying the crossties and showing Augie the picture of Seabiscuit taped to the stall wall. "Did you know Seabiscuit lost his first seventeen races? It's true. Part of it was caused by racing him too young, but the other part was he was running for people rather than himself. When he learned the joy of winning, that's when he set thirteen records. I want you to learn never to let another horse get ahead of you. Sometimes Seabiscuit's jockey would let another horse catch up and then Seabiscuit would really pour it on in the last furlong. Your day is coming, Augie. I will see to it."

By the time Molly prepared Augie's food mixture and cleaned his stall, she could hear Manny's voice herding horses into the big corral. She dusted off her jeans and went out to see her father and Manny filling the hay hoppers. Dancer and Amazing Grace were still saddled and Molly hopped over the railing and began to unfasten the cinches on Grace's saddle.

She used all her strength to pull the saddle off the mare's back and she wrestled it to the top of the railing. She pulled off Grace's saddle blanket and patted her flanks. Now she took time to go over and hug her father. She never removed Dancer's saddle. No matter how tired he was, she would let Manny have that job. Dancer was most used to Manny. When he couldn't see what was happening out his line of vision, Dancer was likely to kick. He was used to Manny's hands and that was fine with Molly.

"So, how was school, young lady?" her father asked. "We sure missed you around here."

"It was hard not to be here. How did the orange tree thing go?"

"I rode Grace over that way. Never in my life have I seen the view you see now. There's a wonderful view of all the new houses across the black top. Now we have to run a fence so the cows don't go over there and stomp down all the seedlings. The government gave us no money for the fencing and it's going to take time to square off two acres."

"You always said not to cry over spilled milk."

"You're right. This will be a good thing some day. Right now, we're going to eat a few thousand dollars. We'll have to deal with it. You can't reverse the canker and that orange grove was ruined whether we liked it or not."

"I thought you going to hit that guy this morning."

"The worst part is I thought so too. I haven't hit anyone since ninth grade, but I could feel my fist tightening into a ball."

"It probably wouldn't have been a good idea, especially with ten of his friends standing there."

"I was mad enough to slug ten office workers, but hitting ten guys who chop down trees for a living might have been more difficult. So, did you meet any new kids at school?"

"I met a boy."

"Oh, oh, first day of junior high and we already have a boyfriend. Manny, I want you to go to school with Molly tomorrow."

"Oh, stop it, Dad. He's just a nice boy who moved here from Baltimore."

"Oh, I see. What's his name?"

"Dan Freeman. He wants to come see the farm someday."

"What would a boy from Baltimore know about a farm?"

"That's the whole point. He'd like to know about the farm. He's only seen a farm twice in his life."

"Yeah, fine with me. When's he coming?"

"Not for a month or so. I told him we have a lot of things going."

"If you like him, I'll like him."

"Molly, it was hard seeing our trees being fed into a machine that ground years of work into a pulp. It isn't like we had a couple orange trees for family use. This is going to hurt us financially, and we'll all have to make sacrifices. If we shave some corners, we should be okay. Molly, we may have to sell some of the livestock."

"What did you say?"

"Don't get all excited."

"What are you saying? We can't sell our livestock."

"Just some of the cows and a few of the lesser horses?"

"And would Augie be considered one of the 'lesser' horses?"

"Of course not. I'm not going to sell your foal, nor would Manny let me part with Dancer or Grace. There are a few, though, that could be sold to the riding stable and a couple more that might get a good price for breeding."

"How many?"

"I talked to Mr. Stuart," Manny said, "He wants the gray and the three quarter horses."

"What's he want them for?" Molly asked.

"The quarter horses for breeding and the gray for his granddaughter. He wants three of the older horses for his riding stable."

"Stuart a slob farmer?" Molly asked, knowing a 'slob' farmer mistreats animals out of laziness or cruelty.

"You shouldn't ask the question, because you should know better. Stuart is a good man and a good rancher. He's paying a fair price and he'd be a fool to mistreat animals he just bought."

"You already sold them?"

"Your father told him it was subject to your approval."

"We need the money?"

"Now we do."

"Sell them," Molly said without hesitation, "I know you can't get too emotional on a farm. What about the cows?"

"What do you think?"

"I think you're sending them to market. You can't have a barbecue without help from the Grimaldis. I wonder if America knows that. When I see people lining up at the fast food places, I can't help but think what they're eating used to live on a farm."

"That's the way it is," Manny offered. "Everything we eat was once alive and that goes for vegetables, fruits, fish, and cattle. We live close to the food sources, but other people just see things on a menu or packaged in a grocery store."

"How many head are we selling?"

"Ten of the Black Angus."

"That'll leave us with twelve horses and twenty or so cows?"

"The good news is we have two pregnant horses and three pregnant cows. Life replaces itself on a farm."

"I know that, Manny," Molly said. "But the other side is that every time we reach down into the things we own, it's a scary time for 3-M. Right now we've lost one third of our oranges, one third of our cows, and almost half of the horses. The births will help, but it won't replace what we had."

"Don't argue with the business woman," Marty Grimaldi said. "Molly knows the bottom line. Here's the way Manny and I see it. If we make these moves now, we'll be money ahead of what we lose. With your approval, we'll buy a new tractor so Manny can double his tomato and onion crops and give us a new cash source. I have my eye on a half dozen horses that Bauer may sell if he sells his farm and we're right back in it by next spring."

"Dad," Molly said abruptly, "will you teach me how to ride the Dancer?"

"That's a big change in subject. Let's stay with one thing at a time. Do you agree with the sales we have to make?'

"Yes I agree. I want to spend some time with the horses and cattle before they go, but, yes, I know we have to do what we have to do. I'm just surprised we're doing it so quickly."

"You know ranchers and farmers don't have the luxury of waiting for things to happen. Ranchers have to make things happen."

"If you and Manny say to sell, I say you must be right. So, will you help me learn to ride the Dancer?"

"Why do you want to ride Dancer? He's big and dangerous. A big old stallion like Dancer is very unpredictable. I don't even ride him too often. Manny rides him, but Manny was a jockey. Why don't you just ride Grace?"

"I want to ride her, too. I want Augie to see me riding other horses. I want him to see that horses are to be ridden."

"He'll be jealous," Manny said.

"You bet he will," Molly said, smiling a sneaky smile. "I'm thinking he won't like that at all. Then, when his time comes, he might be more than ready for me to ride him."

"What does that have to do with riding Dancer?"

"That's a whole different plan," Molly said. "Are you going to teach me or not?"

"I'll let Manny work with you on that one. I want you to remember a stallion is different than a riding horse. You never get on Dancer until both Manny and I are with you. If he takes off we don't have another horse that can catch him. With two horses, we could cut him off."

"I intend to stay in the big corral."

"Yeah," Manny said. "But you've never seen Dancer jump. If he senses you're an amateur he could take you over the fence and halfway to downtown Ocala."

"I better make friends with him first."

"Thoroughbreds don't have many friends," Manny said.

CHAPTER EIGHT

A Boy From Baltimore

Molly learned to get up forty-five minutes early to put on coffee and finish her homework. By the time Manny showed up at the house, Marty Grimaldi would be frying bacon and Molly would finish getting ready for school. Just before running the driveway toward the bus stop, she'd feed and talk to Augie and nowadays she'd take two carrots and feed them to Dashaway Dancer. The Dancer seemed confused by this new friendship, but he wasn't about to turn down carrots early in the morning. The same horse that used to snort when Molly passed now hung his head over his stall and kicked to get her attention. The plan was going nicely.

Another thing going nicely was her relationship with Danny. Already Danny saved Molly a seat on the bus each morning and their conversations were free-flowing. He told her all about city life and Molly countered with what it was like to live on a farm. In vocal music class, Danny was amazing. He had a great voice and he could read music. Most of the other students had to learn songs line by line, but Danny would hum the song from the sheet music and seemed always be on perfect pitch. The other girls did everything possible to get Danny's attention, but by the end of each hour he maneuvered his way back to Molly's side. They were friends. He opened doors and sat with her at lunch. There weren't any poses or mind games. Danny was just Danny. In fact, Danny was just dandy.

In a few weeks she'd invite Danny for dinner and she already spoke to her father and Manny and informed them they had better be on their best behaviors. Probably the best idea might be to invite Karen Cable and Manny's lady friend who worked on Mr. Stuart's farm and they could all have a barbe-

cue. That way, if Danny became uncomfortable, the two of them could escape to the barn or they could go riding.

Danny was an incredibly good listener who would rather talk about events and other people than himself. He really paid attention because he often asked follow-up questions.

"So," he asked one day on the way home from school. "You already know I'm jealous that you live on a farm, but I bet you also know I probably don't know what I'm talking about. I bet there's a lot of work to do, huh?"

"There are only three human beings most of the time on the farm and we have to do everything that gets done. We hire other people when it's time to harvest the oranges, but most of the other stuff we do."

"Like what?"

"Wow, where do I start? We make our own food and only buy the things we can't make or grow. We have to care for the horses, the cows, the chickens, the groves, the gardens, the hay, the branding, the vaccinations, the tractors and vehicles, and the upkeep of the farm."

"You know how to do all that stuff?"

"Most of it. My dad and Manny give me lots of breaks when I'm in school and they help with the cooking and the laundry. During summer and vacations, those are my jobs."

"Don't you hate it sometimes?"

"I don't guess so. It's not like I used to live in a neighborhood and then moved to a farm. It's all I've ever known."

"Do you get jealous?"

"No, I really don't. I mean, I love some of the beautiful homes with the swimming pools and all and I guess I'd like to have fewer chores, but I don't know if I can explain how I feel. I think it's like city people are connected to each other and farm people are connected to the land."

"I think I understand."

"Okay," Molly said, her eyes wider. "I think I've found the right explanation. When I walk under the 3-M sign when we get off this bus, I walk right back into another century. It's like another age, a different time, and it's a time and age I like better than I guess what others would call the real world. In my world, horses and cows are important, the weather means success or failure, and the ground is never something you grass over just to mow down. I like bonfires instead of fireplaces. I like the smell of hay over flowers. I prefer sunsets to television. I talk to horses more than people. I'd rather sit on the porch and listen to night sounds rather than canned sounds from radio and television. I hate dressing up and it's obvious I don't like makeup and stuff. All of that makes me kind of a nut, huh?"

"Not at all, Molly," Danny said. "I'm just really angry I couldn't have met you later than now."

"What?"

"Never mind. It was a stupid thing to say."

"Come on, Danny," Molly pushed. "What does that mean? You're sorry you met me?"

"I knew I was in trouble the moment I said that. It's a compliment, Molly. I'm happy to know you now, but I wish it could be later. Please let me explain it another time. You are really the only real friend I've met since I came here. I just really like all the stuff you were saying about the sunsets and bonfires and I think I just said out loud what I was thinking. Is it okay if I don't explain it right now?"

"Sure, I guess so."

"Look Molly. It's your stop."

"You're happy to get rid of me?"

"Yeah, before I put my other foot in my mouth. Yep, have a nice day. See you tomorrow, Molly."

"I'm not dropping this."

"I figured you wouldn't. I'm just happy to get off the hook today."

"Danny, remind me to talk to you about something else."

"What?"

"In a week or so, you want to come to a picnic on the farm?"

"Yeah, I'd like that."

Molly bounced down the stairs of the bus and didn't have to turn around to know Danny would watch her until the bus started down the road to let the rich kids off at the subdivisions. Danny was great. Molly pulled down the latch of the mailbox and pulled out a collection of bills and flyers. The Grimaldis even got different mail than Danny's family did. They probably got mail from fancy department stores and up-scale restaurants. The Grimaldis got mail advertising tractors and new kinds of feed and nutrients for crops and animals. Molly walked under the big wooden 3-M sign and into another time.

CHAPTER NINE

New Love and Perfect Presents

When Molly first saw the Bronco she became excited, but then she remembered Doc Cable was gone and Karen owned it now. As she reached the house to put her books down she could hear laughter in the kitchen. Sure enough, Karen and Marty were enjoying coffee. Molly hugged both of them. She noted that they seemed to be acting guilty. Both of them looked like teenagers who had just been caught at something.

"Molly," Karen Cable said, "you are likely the prettiest girl in this whole area."

"Oh, stop it. You know you are."

"Well, thank you. But my time is fleeting, aged that I am. Now, every year you look better, I'll likely look a little worse."

"I doubt that," Marty Grimaldi added. "I'm thinking the best looking women in this entire county are in this kitchen right this second."

"Dad, let's stop this now. We're the most beautiful women in the world and you are the most handsome man on earth. How are you, Karen?"

"I'm feeling better every day. I miss my dad, but now I've gone through his things and I'm trying to get out to check up on all his patients. I was waiting for you so we can visit that foal of yours. The other day I bought a portable X-ray machine that will give us a picture of that bone."

"You're kidding?"

"I take the slides here and then I can analyze them back at the office. It's a state-of-the-art machine that my father would never have ordered. It'll pay for itself over time. We won't have to guess about your horse's leg. We take slides now and repeat the process every six months. My dad was great at just using his experience to make judgments about interior wounds. I don't have his experience so I let medical technology help me."

"But soon you'll have experience and technology."

"I will, won't I? Then I just have to deal with men who view a woman vet the way they do a woman running for the presidency of the United States. Isn't that right, Marty?"

"Come on, Karen. I was just saying that Dancer was very skittish and it would be wise to let Manny and I hold him in crossties while you examine him."

"Did you and Manny hold him down when my father examined him?"

"No."

"I rest my case. Molly, go change and we'll go have a look at that horse of yours. In the meantime, the little girl vet is going to look at those mean old big horses and your daddy will help me if I get scared."

"Come on, Karen," Marty Grimaldi said as he and Karen headed for the barn. "I was just saying that Dancer has an attitude problem."

"Sure, Marty. But if clients do not see men and women vets as equal, I'll be out of business."

Molly recognized that her father had the same look on his face as Danny did when they met and talked on the school bus. She was sure something was going on between her father and Karen. She smiled as she pulled on her jeans.

By the time Molly reached the barn Karen had already checked out Amazing Grace and now she held Dashaway Dancer's huge head in her hands. There was no one else holding the stallion and Karen yelled at him to hold still while she pulled his lips back to look at his teeth. Dancer snorted but held still. Karen looked in his ears and then she stared into his eyes. Holding him firmly, she shoved a needle into his withers. Dancer winced.

"One of the finest animals I've seen," Karen said and she patted Dancer's face and reached in her jeans pocket to get him a sugar cube, "That's a big boy. Did Karen give you a little shot and you liked it, huh? You just got a booster filled with vitamins and other things you needed, old buddy. Next time I see you, you'll get an apple and nothing else. How's that? I don't want you thinking I only bring things that hurt. We need to be buddies and I want you to remember me for sugar and apples, too. Marty, this is a fine stallion. Why aren't you running him?"

"Broken spirit."

"Oh yeah, my dad told me the story. Spirit gets bent—not broken. You tried to run him?"

"Manny takes him out every now and then. He's as fast as a scalded dog until another horse runs with him."

"What happens then?"

"He breaks stride and slows right down. He's a broken man, so we just use him for breeding."

"I'll just mind my business on this one," Karen said. "You could be wrong, you know?"

"He is wrong," Molly said, making her presence known. "Dad's given up on him. Manny said Dancer is as fast as he ever was—maybe faster. Dad doesn't like Manny running him because he'll just get his heart broken if he races again."

"Molly, you know that's not true. We put him in with Amazing Grace and even she beat him."

"You used the wrong horse," Molly said.

"What?"

"A man wouldn't understand, huh Karen?"

"I think I might understand what you mean. Let's have a look at your horse. Marty, hook up that white machine with a long cord and bring those negative plates over here by the stall."

"Wait a minute. What are you two saying a man wouldn't understand?"

"Never mind," Karen said, "Just get the black plates. Darn, look at this horse. Oh Molly, he's beautiful. I wish I brought the scales. I bet he's over two hundred pounds already. What's this girl feeding you, Handsome?"

"I call him..." Molly said and stopped.

"I know you call him Augie," Karen said, suddenly turning to face Molly. "Is it okay I don't call him that name just yet?"

"Karen, I'm so sorry."

"Oh, don't you be sorry. My father was so thrilled you named your horse after him. Now that I see him up close, it was a magnificent tribute. Every day I live with my father's things and I have to use his notes in order to know which farmers and ranchers I need to visit. It's hard sometimes."

Suddenly Karen Cable began to cry and Molly crowded into Augie's stall to hug her. Handsome Augie was confused, not only to have a stranger in his stall hugging the only human he loved, but he had never heard crying before and it was a sound that made him tilt his head and stare at both of the women. He appeared to be so concerned that Karen looked at him and burst out laughing.

"Oh Handsome," she said to the foal as she offered a lump of sugar. "Don't try to understand women. I'll call you by the right name soon enough. Someday, I'll be proud to say your name out loud. Okay?"

"What's going on here?" Marty asked. "Everything okay?"

"All is well," Karen said, turning away and wiping at her face. "You all plugged in?"

"I asked if something was wrong."

"What's wrong is I have a nosy helper. I need the black plates here and you and Molly out of the barn. I'm going to hook up the plates in back and front of Handsome's leg and push some buttons from outside the window. It's like at the dentist's office when you get X-rays."

It didn't take long before Karen put the black slides in a light-proof box and took them out to the Bronco. She explained that the slides would be developed back at the office and she would call later in the evening to report the status of Augie's leg. Marty and Molly packed up the machine and now Karen took a longer look at Handsome Augie. It was immediately clear she had more knowledge than her father and she tested things her father never had. She even used a microscope to look at test slides of blood and saliva samples and Augie watched her and sniffed at her long black hair as she peered into the lens of the microscope.

"This is a tremendously healthy horse," she said finally. "Every test comes back at the high end of normal. You've done beautifully, Molly. Handsome is a beautiful specimen. Your Dashaway Dancer is the most perfect stallion I've ever seen and this horse may be even better. You looking to race him some day?"

"I think about it, but your dad said he should never race because of his leg."

"Ever hear of Glenn Cunningham?"

"No."

"Glenn Cunningham had polio as a boy and walked with legs braces until he was eight years old. Against his mother's and doctor's wishes, he shed the braces and put himself on a running program. He ran every day and night until he was faster than any boy in town."

"Yeah?"

"Glenn Cunningham became the first man to run a mile in under four minutes."

"So, you disagree with your father's advice?"

"Only to the degree that Cunningham was a man and Handsome is a horse. Glenn could decide on his own program and you have to decide what's best for a horse."

"Karen," Marty said, "this is a time I agree with your father. Augie could crumble under his own weight. Maybe it's better he's saved for breeding."

"You don't believe in him like you don't believe in Dancer."

"I'm not going to argue. I just think I do things on the safe side."

"Then you should buy a boat and refuse to take it out in the lake. You never know when there could be a storm or the engine might break down. You could put it in a nice safe garage and go in and look at it. A boat like yours would look brand new and you could half of its worth once you're done looking at it."

"I get the point, but I'm not a risk taker."

"You don't say."

"You are really sarcastic, aren't you?"

"I'm sorry. I was just pointing out that you need to keep your alternatives open. My father was a brilliant man and he might turn out to be right about your horse. The problem I have with what you're saying is that you've written off this foal like you have your stallion. Handsome won't even be able to be ridden for another year, and already you close the door on his possibilities. My father was a smart man and no one loved him more than I did, but he's also the same man who said women are better teachers than they are vets."

"Your father said that?" Molly asked.

"Isn't it hysterical? I laughed so hard. In my father's head women are good to work with people's children, but maybe they shouldn't be trusted with their animals. Isn't that a stitch?"

"That's not what he was saying," Marty Grimaldi protested.

"Oh, yes it was," Karen said and now both women laughed. "He was saying that women should stay in the places where we're used to seeing them. A woman could be a teacher and help a first grader with her shoes, but that same woman should never put shoes on a horse. I love you and my dad, but you need to join this century. You just might have a woman president in your future, Mr. Grimaldi. What do you think of that?"

"I think we should go out and have a pizza."

"What does that have to do with what Karen said?" Molly asked.

"It means there is no good answer to what Karen said. Whatever I would have said, you girls would have jumped on it. I took the pizza defense. I'll find Manny and see if he wants to come along."

Karen continued to fawn over Handsome Augie and Molly couldn't believe how beautiful she was. Karen had perfect features, was tall and slim, but it was her black hair and shining dark eyes that made her look spectacular. She could be a model. She made good choices. It was obvious she didn't back down from anyone. And she was an expert on every critter on the ranch. The relationship between Karen and Marty was going to be fun to watch. Marty was certainly interested in Karen and for him to offer to take them out for pizza was rare. If Manny came along with them the farm would be untended for a few hous and that almost never happened.

As it turned out Manny stayed at home to clean the tack room and brush the horses they were about to sell, but it was likely he wanted to call his girlfriend. Manny wanted his private life completely private.

Molly rode with Karen and Marty followed behind in the jeep. This two car arrangement would allow Karen to go directly home from the restaurant rather than driving Molly and Marty back to the ranch. Molly was surprised at how fast Karen drove, and they listened to the same music. Together, they could drive her father and Manny crazy. Molly played video games until the pizza came and allowed her father to have some private time with Karen.

When they left the restaurant, Molly jumped in the jeep and let her father flirt with Karen at the rear of her Bronco. Just as he began walking back to the jeep with a little smile on his face, Karen leaped into the Bronco, beeped the horn and motioned for him to come to the passenger side. Now he was carrying a box to the jeep. Karen shouted to Molly, "Hey, kid. The stuff in the box is for you. I thought you might like it."

Incredibly, before calling it a night, there were still chores and homework to do. Molly tossed the box on her bed and dashed out to the barn to give Augie a quick brushing, sneak a few carrots to Dancer, and make sure the cows and chickens were fed. It was a quick night for Augie, but she planned to spend lots of time with him this weekend. She dashed back into the house and started a load of laundry before sitting down at the kitchen table to finish her math and answer some questions for government class. Her father and Manny were putting the farm to bed and the moon was rising huge and orange from the east. Then the phone rang.

"Oh, Karen," Molly said into the phone. "I don't even know where my dad is, but I could go beep the jeep horn and see if he comes."

"I was calling to talk to you, Molly. I've looked at the X-rays."

"Already?"

"Yes, and the break looks totally healed. Isn't that great?"

"So, he's perfectly fine?"

"No, don't hear things I didn't say. The bone is healed, but there's a layer of calcium ringing the bone. I don't think the bone is calcified. I think the ring surrounds the bone but isn't part of it."

"You're losing me."

"Okay, let me break this down. Handsome's bone is healed. There are no chips or spurs and that's good. It's also true, though, that even an X-ray can determine whether there's calcium mixed in with the bone. The bone is solid, but the ring around it makes it difficult to tell if there isn't some calcium filling in cracks. Calcium isn't as strong as bone, but it's the best we could hope for—does that make sense?"

"I think so. You're saying there's no danger for him to run on it."

"Yep, that's what I'm saying for now. A year from now, when he carries the weight of a rider, we'll take another look."

"So there's still some risk?"

"No, not for the next year there isn't. This is good, Molly. You trust me on this."

"I trust you completely."

"Did you open the box?"

"Gee, I forgot. Should I open it with you on the phone?"

"No way. I want you to open it in private. There are a few things there I just thought my dad would want you to have. My father loved you very much."

"And I love him very much."

"Present tense?"

"My love for your father will always be present tense."

"Nicely said, Ms. Grimaldi. Tell your father I'll talk to him soon."

Molly wanted to ask whether Karen was interested in Mr. Grimaldi, but Molly had learned not to corner people, and, anyway, Karen's interest was obvious and her father was like a junior high boy any time Karen was around. Molly cleaned the kitchen counter, made three lunches, and headed for her room. She heard her father come in and came out to kiss him good night and thank him for the pizza. She told him about Karen's call and soon heard him sneak out on the porch to smoke his pipe and talk to Karen on the phone. It was all so very cute.

Back in her room Molly pulled tape off of the cardboard box. Gently, she pulled back the flaps and the first thing she saw was an eight-by-ten picture of Doctor August Cable that must have been taken at his seventieth birthday and, birthday or not, he wore his floppy cowboy hat and one pant leg was hanging over his boot. He was blowing out a sea of birthday candles and it was wonderful to see him again—even in a picture. Molly didn't have any pictures of Doc and she'd buy a frame and treasure this one. Still in the box, there was a yellowed newspaper wrapping something about the same size as the photo. Molly tenderly unwrapped the ancient newspaper and there was another photo and this one was in a frame. "Oh, my goodness!" Here it was. Doc had talked about this, but Molly thought it might be just a story. She stared at the picture and here was Doc dressed in jockey silks and atop a beautiful stallion in the winner's circle under a sign that read 'Churchill Downs.' He was young and thin and he was the winner he said he was. Now Molly picked up the ancient newspaper and read:

May 2, 1952 - Up and coming jockey August W. Cable sits atop Mountain Boy as the two enjoy first honors in the fifth running of the 'Pick-Three' sweepstakes. A ten to one underdog, Cable took Mountain Boy along the rail and won by three lengths. Cable has already placed in the money six of nine times and is a candidate for "Jockey of the Year."

All of Doc's stories were true! This was just great. In the past, Molly had listened to Doc's stories and thought he might be like the old war veterans who told stories that might be more myth than fact. Doc was the real deal. There was one more thing in the box, but Molly doubted anything could beat what she had already seen. She reached into the box a last time and this time there was something wrapped in a thick layer of bubble wrap. She carefully removed the scotch tape holding the wrap together and instantly began to cry. She looked at the picture and then back to her bed, and now she knew these were the actual silks Augie Cable had worn the day he won the big race. She held up the silks, faded blue and red, and now a jockey's cap fell on the bed. Inside was a small note written by Doc himself: "These go to Molly Grimaldi. Molly, you wear these someday and know I'll be watching." Now Molly cried and tears rolled down her cheeks and onto the silks. The pictures had come from Karen, but the silks and hat came from Doc himself. Had Augie already been born when Doc wrote the note? Did Doc know he would die soon? Was Karen sad because Doc had given the silks to a little girl down the road?

Molly woke the next morning, still dressed from the day before, and Doc's silks felt sleek and warm against her face. The lights had been turned off, so her father must have seen the silks.

CHAPTER TEN

Losing Friends and Making Plans

For a girl on a farm, weekends were particularly wonderful. Even though the weekend was the same as any other days for her father and Manny, on Saturdays and Sundays Molly slept in until nine and then took on her chores with less fury than was necessary during the week. On Saturdays she swept and mopped both the kitchen and the front porch. She most often would put a roast or brisket in the crock pot to let them cook slowly all day and then she had most of the two days to catch up on homework, practice her singing, and, of course, spend time with Handsome Augie. This Saturday, however, she changed her routine and went out to the barn and saddled up Amazing Grace. She stopped at Dancer's stall and fed him three carrots, said a quick morning greeting to Augie, and then she leaped atop Grace's back and was sure to duck her head as she went under the doorway.

She was sure that Augie was furious and she purposely took Grace for a long ride out in the east pasture and all the way to the fence that protected the new orange tree seedlings. She worked Grace into a canter and then a near gallop and the palomino raced parallel to the road and passersby pointed at the girl whose long blonde hair flowed behind her in perfect harmony with Grace's golden mane dancing on the wind. Molly's fanny was up in the air and Amazing Grace glided and stretched and the feeling was always a great experience. Now Molly praised Grace and walked her slowly toward the corral to cool her out so as not to tighten her muscles. Grace was spent. She hadn't run so hard in a very long time. Now Molly was almost ready to get Augie. She hoped he was good and angry right now. He ought to be.

Tying Grace off in the small corral, Molly stopped off at the house to turn her roast and grab a few apples. She often had to remind herself to eat and she ate a protein bar and headed back out to the barn. By the time she arrived, the other horses were out in the west pasture. Her father and Manny were nowhere to be seen. Because it was Saturday, it was most likely they were riding fence and making sure the irrigation pumps were flowing freely. Only weather and unexpected events changed the schedule ,and there was no such thing as a day off. Molly walked in the barn and immediately heard Augie kicking his stall walls and snorting. Still Molly took her time going to him. She swept and cleaned two stalls before heading in his direction.

"Someone feeling a little neglected this morning?" she asked her horse. Augie shook his head up and down as if he were nodding. "Well, we can't always be the only show in town, can we? I'm thinking this apple might make a foal feel better. Yeah, that's pretty good, huh? Let's put this bridle on and we'll go see a real horse."

Molly walked Augie out to the little corral and took off the lead and let him go. Immediately Augie walked over to his mother and tried to nurse. Grace pushed him away and the second time Augie approached she took a nip near Augie's ears. Molly smiled as Augie took off for the other side of the corral. Now Molly untied Grace and jumped up on the palomino's back. Augie stared. This was something he had never seen before and he tilted his head like he was trying to understand. Now Molly and Grace began to move. Augie followed them. Each time he nearly caught up, Molly would nudge Grace's sides to quicken her pace. Soon Molly had Grace canter and still Augie followed and tried to keep up. Molly hugged the split rail fence and soon Grace and Augie cantered easily along the rail following the circular pattern racing horses learn. Until now Augie ran a random path around the corral, but now he was learning discipline and following pattern.

Molly also wanted Augie to see being ridden was an honor and if being ridden was praise for his mother, some day it would be praise for him. Augie was very jealous and several times nipped at his mother's tail. Molly knew horses are much like children and Augie would be motivated to excel by her praising another horse.

Molly took Grace back to the barn first and put her in her freshly cleaned stall. She rubbed the palomino down with a towel and Grace loved the attention. Molly was pleased her father made no mention of selling Grace. Molly understood that palominos were tremendously popular and Grace would have commanded the price of three other horses. She was in her prime and, next to Dancer; she was the finest of Grimaldi stock. She was beautiful and calm, easy to ride, and perfect for breeding. Although her father might have considered letting Grace go, Molly knew that facing her and Manny afterward would not have been worth any price.

Back out in the corral, Augie was running the same path he had just learned. If it weren't for his leg, Augie would be the most valuable of all Grimaldi horses. He was only four months old and could have a tremendous future. His breeding was perfect and his lines resembled War Admiral's. He was going to be a very big boy—maybe sixteen to eighteen hands high—and now he pranced as if he knew he was special.

Once Augie saw Molly watching him from the rail he immediately cut the corral in half and ran to her. Molly wrestled his head in her arms and playfully boxed his ears. She opened the gate and practiced walking backward in front of him and motioning with her fingers for him to follow. She watched his legs. He walked evenly. He watched her hands as she moved. This was a smart horse. The moment Molly held her hands in a stop motion; Augie froze in his tracks until she started moving her fingers and began walking again. There was so much to do. Molly couldn't forget that Augie needed her every day.

He needed to depend on her. He needed to know who was boss.

That Sunday Molly parted her curtains and saw four huge trucks pulling onto Grimaldi land. They were not from the county this time. This was worse. Molly took her shower and slipped on fresh jeans and a checkered blouse and again went to the window. She saw the quarter horses being loaded on one truck and the grey and breeding horses being loaded on the other. It was a sickening sight to see her horses being loaded to live in another place. She wondered if any of them understood what was happening. It was clear Manny was upset. He looked smaller than usual, and he dabbed at his eyes with a multicolored hanky as his friends walked up planks and were tied with crossties for the ride to Stuart's farm. Manny had helped bring most of these horses into this world. He had fed and watered and loved them every day of their lives. With pigs, cows, and chickens it was different because these animals go to market, so it was easy to try to stay unattached. With horses it was impossible not to be attached. Each one had a unique personality and Manny knew and loved every one. He looked around to see if anyone was watching. His face showed incredible pain and he turned away from the trucks and vigorously wiped at his eyes.

The moment the two trucks carrying the horses headed down the road toward the blacktop, the other two trucks moved into position next to the chute. Marty was out in the pen and counting up to ten. Apparently there were three cows too many and he pushed three out into the east pasture. Molly wondered if he saved specific cows or just pushed any three to safety. One by one the cows walked through the chute and crowded onto the trucks for a final ride. Molly hoped the cows had no idea where they were going.

Lunch was very quiet and it was good Molly had elected to cook fish taken from the pond and vegetables from Manny's garden. She introduced the idea of a picnic and said she wanted to invite Danny Freeman. There was no teasing. She picked a good day. Marty and Manny said they would invite their girlfriends. The rest of the lunch was eaten in uncomfortable silence.

Finally Marty spoke, "Still work to do, Manny."

"You bet, boss," Manny replied, taking his plate to the sink, and disappearing outside.

"Molly," Marty said, "we have to stay in business. We have to make hard decisions. Today we got to stay in business a while longer."

"Dad, I understand we did what we needed to do. Some people are losing their ranches and farms all at once. We have to stay alive."

The Grimaldis hugged in the middle of the kitchen and Molly could feel her father sighing heavily. She hugged him harder. They separated. Marty Grimaldi placed his plate in the sink. Then he fished hundred dollar bills out of his jean pocket and threw them on the counter like they were empty candy wrappers. There was no doubt Marty Grimaldi preferred animals over money. Molly put the money in the coffee can above the sink as usual. The bills would be paid but the horses and cows would still be gone. Marty Grimaldi would not rest until they were all replaced.

CHAPTER ELEVEN

The Ultimate First Dance

The Grimaldi house and farm was the culmination of four generations of love and hard work. Great grandfather built it 40 feet by 40 feet square with wood and stone walls that shone in the morning sun. Grandfather added a huge porch that ran the 40 feet across the front of the house and 15 feet deep. Twenty neighboring farmers added the huge barn in a 'barn raising' one summer when Marty was a boy. Marty made the beautifully crafted mahogany porch swing when Molly was just a baby. Someday Molly wanted to build kennels to raise dogs and care for pets whose owners needed or wanted to be out of town. She planned to be a vet, so kenneling was a natural side business to be in which could also help 3-M Farm stay in business. Hundreds of times Molly looked at what her ancestors had built. She vowed she would never let the Grimaldi homestead and farm slip into other hands.

The farm was the perfect location for a picnic and Karen Cable arrived early in the morning to help shuck corn and ready the barbecue pit. Manny brought his girlfriend Rosalee. She was chunky and cute and spoke mostly Spanish. Even though Marty offered to help build them a cabin next to Manny's bunkhouse, it didn't seem like Manny and Rosalee ever would get married. They were fun to watch, though. They clearly enjoyed being with each other. Marty and Karen were comfortable with one another too. Once her father kissed Karen's cheek when he delivered foil wrapped potatoes to put on the fire. Molly figured these two just might get married.

Around noon a late model car dropped Danny off at the gate, and Molly drove the jeep down to pick him up.

"Hey Molly!" Danny shouted, "You're driving!"

"Hi Dan. Thanks for coming. I've been driving the jeep since I was eleven, but just on the farm. One day my dad and Manny forgot their lunches way out on the east end, so I drove out there. At first my dad was mad, but now I can bring them lunch that's still hot. I still grind the gears every now and then. Jump in and I'll show you the ranch."

"This is great," Danny said. "You drive a car. That's so cool. I guess you can do that on a farm. Now, what is this—a farm or a ranch?"

"We call it a farm, but when you have cattle you can call it a ranch. I guess it's both. You nervous about meeting my dad?"

"Are you kidding? He looks like a guy right out of an action western, but I wasn't going to turn this down. You own all this?"

"A little over forty acres," Molly said. "The house is smack in the middle, so I'll take you around the whole perimeter."

Molly bounced the jeep into the pasture and Danny made 'mooing' sounds as they passed the cows. He was definitely a city boy. Then Molly showed him the pond and told him how it not only watered the cattle but that her father had added catfish and bass. Now some of them were big enough to eat."

"Could we go fishing after lunch?"

"Sure, if you want to. The catfish won't bite during the day, but we'll catch a few bass."

"You're kidding. I've only been fishing twice in my life."

"Well then, we'll have to go. We just had some of the catfish the other day."

"Catfish are good to eat?"

"Oh Danny, catfish are very good—very sweet. I'll send a package home with you and write directions so your mom will know how to cook them."

"How about the bass?"

"I like catching them, but I don't like the taste."

"I still can't believe your father lets you drive a car. You're only thirteen."

"The jeep isn't a car, really," Molly said as she rounded the pond. "I guess you do things earlier on a farm. I was milking cows at about six and riding horses by the time I was seven. Then when my mom died I had to take over all the inside stuff like cooking and cleaning."

"Molly, I never know what to say about your mom."

"There's nothing to say and nothing for you to feel uncomfortable about, Danny. Really. My dad says we play the cards we're dealt. I'm playing mine as best I can. Look over here. Across this fence used to be an orange grove. See the little seedlings? That's what they left us."

"Who?" Danny asked, assuming the subject of Molly's mother was ended. "Who cut down the trees?"

"The county. Florida has a citrus canker disease that destroys the outside of the oranges. The inside is still good, but they say to kill the disease they have to cut down the trees. They're cutting trees from here to Boca Raton."

"Where's that?"

"On the coast near Lauderdale. Anyway, they cut the trees and put them in a chipper and we had to sell some horses and cows to make up the loss. Anyway, that's what we have left. Let's zoom over to the west meadow and then we'll head in for lunch. You doing okay so far?"

"Having a ball," Danny said.

Molly shifted the jeep into first gear and then shifted into second like a pro. Danny was impressed. As they picked up speed Molly's hair flew into Danny and he smelled how fresh and clean it was. He couldn't help but look at her. The fact she had no clue she was the most beautiful girl at school made her all the more beautiful.

"Why are we stopping?"

"My hair was whipping at you," Molly said, reaching into her pocket for a rubber band and gathering her long golden blonde hair into a ponytail. "I should have banded it before we started riding. I wanted to show you how the subdivisions look to us. See that row of houses past our fence line? Those came in just over two years ago. There was dust everywhere and when the dust cleared those houses were there. The land used to be old man Kelly's farm. My dad says two thirds of the farms will be gone in ten years or less. I guess that's progress."

"No, it isn't."

"So, tell me about Baltimore," Molly said, "I don't want to bore you with all this."

"This isn't boring at all. It's great."

"Everything is how you look at it. Farming is nonstop work. You have to love the land so much you're willing to do anything. I think it's in the blood...so, will you tell me about Baltimore?"

"Oh, Baltimore," Danny said. "I told you I've lived in several places. Baltimore was cool, I guess. What I did like is that Baltimore is close to lots of neat places. I got to see New York City and the Statue of Liberty and where The World Trade Center used to be."

"Wow."

"Yeah, I got to see the White House, Arlington National Cemetery, the Smithsonian, and I went to Camden Yard to watch the Orioles play."

"You got to do all that?'

"Yeah, Baltimore's in the middle of everything, so I got to see a lot of things."

"I haven't seen any of those things. Did you ever see Niagara Falls?"

"Twice. Once from the American side and once from the Canadian side."

"You're kidding?"

"Molly, I'd rather learn how to drive this jeep. You heard what I said. City kids go to places to look at stuff. We look at it and then we go look at something else. You do stuff. That's better."

"I don't know. I'd like to see all those things you mentioned. We never leave the farm for too long. Even if we had the money, we couldn't go away for a week."

"Yeah, but don't you get it? People from the cities can leave because no one misses them or totally depends on them while they're gone? Couldn't you get your hired hand to watch the farm while you and your dad went on vacation?"

"Manny isn't a hired hand. Manny is a partner."

"I didn't mean that in a nasty way."

"I know, but Manny is family and if we went on vacation, he should go too. I was just saying someday I'd like to see all those neat things. You getting hungry?"

"I'm starved," Danny said. "But you should have let me bring something."

"Danny, there's so much food, it's almost ridiculous. My dad loves to barbecue and he took out these humongous steaks and then there's Rosa's salad, and potatoes, and corn, and Karen baked a huge cake. Get the picture?"

Molly pulled the jeep in behind Karen's Bronco. Immediately Danny was bombarded with introductions. Molly liked the way he handled himself. In minutes Molly's father was showing him the famous swing and how his great grandfather used dowels instead of nails in building the house. Acting like he had known these people a long while, Danny joked with Manny and asked Rosa about the things in her salad that he'd never seen before. She explained mostly in Spanish and Danny flashed a smile toward Molly that said he had no idea what she was saying. Karen glided over to tell Molly her boyfriend was big-time handsome. Molly knew it was no use to try to deny Danny was her boyfriend. He was a charmer. He repeatedly walked over to the stone front of the house and felt the stones. He was impressed and knew how to impress others.

"Your grandfather built this himself?"

"My great grandfather. My grandfather built the porch. My dad built the swing. There will be a quiz on all this. Dan, come on over and help me get these steaks going."

After Danny had eaten most of his huge steak, two ears of corn, a helping of Rosa's salad, and a big piece of cake, Marty asked, "What else can I get for you?"

"A stretcher if I eat another thing. That was the best meal I've ever eaten. I guess Molly got me hungry zooming around in the jeep."

"Did she scare you?" Karen asked.

"Only about thirty times. She jumped over a ridge and I turned around to look for my kidneys. I'm kidding. She's a good driver. Now let me help clean up. This meal was great."

"Nope," Karen said. "You kids haven't seen a good friend of Molly's yet."

"I get to meet Augie?"

"Yep, and then I'll take you fishing."

"We going in the jeep?"

"No, Sir," Molly said. "We'll be riding horses out to the pond."

"You're kidding? I've never ridden a horse."

"In that case," Manny said, "make sure you saddle up the Dancer and he'll give Danny a nice gentle ride." Everyone laughed uproariously except Danny and Manny continued, "Oh yes, my new friend, Dancer is very gentle and he loves to go on a nice Sunday afternoon ride."

"What's so funny?" Danny asked, as even Molly's face was red.

"Dancer is a stallion and he'd kill you, Danny. Even I don't ride him. I just pictured you getting on his back and flying off. He'd take you for the ride of a lifetime. You'll see why it's funny when I show you the Dancer."

"How come everyone says 'the' before Dancer?" Danny asked, "I mean, you all say 'The Dancer'."

"It's kind of like when you say 'the Babe', or 'the Pope'," Manny said. "The Dancer is a race horse and he commands respect. You'll see what I mean."

Molly ran into the house and returned with an armful of apples and soon she and Danny headed out toward the barn. They were a cute couple and Marty Grimaldi took a long look at his little girl who wasn't so little any more. Karen seemed to know what he was thinking and moved over to touch his arm. "You've given her a good upbringing, Marty. She'll be fine."

"She's just growing up so fast and the hardest years are just beginning."

"Like I said, you did just fine. You'll see."

Out in the barn Molly and Danny stood in front of Dashaway Dancer's stall. The Dancer was in rare form and kicked at his stall wall and was snorting as he looked at the new person in the Grimaldi barn. He raised and lowered his great head and he snorted as if he was not at all impressed with Danny. Molly fished an apple out of her shirt and tried to hand it to Danny.

"Oh, you're kidding," Danny said. "He's huge. I never thought a horse could be so big. You guys ride a horse like this?"

"I don't," Molly said. "I know my limitations. I never used to even get close to him, but I've been working on him lately."

"He looks mean."

"Dad says he has an attitude problem—kind of a juvenile delinquent. The truth is, he's high strung."

"He sure is."

Now Dancer put on a show. He was rearing and kicking and his ears were laid back. His tail stood out in a bristle and he nodded up and down. Danny backed away and Molly moved forward.

"Oh, knock it off," Molly said. She produced an apple. "Is this what all that nonsense was about? You knew I'd bring you an apple and you have to show off. Okay, you're a big bad boy and everyone is supposed to be afraid of you. Now calm down or you get nothing. That's a big boy."

Danny was frozen in place and was amazed this lovely girl could calm a giant like the Dancer. Now the same horse that was so menacing gently took an apple in his lips and soon the juice ran down the sides of his mouth. Molly patted him while he ate and he nuzzled at her shirt for a second apple. Soon she produced a second apple, teased him with it by moving her hand side to side and then she let him take it gently from her fingers.

"I'm working on him," Molly said to Danny. "He's just a big baby."

"He's the biggest baby I've ever seen," Danny said, hugging the opposite wall past Dancer's stall. "I'm not riding a horse that big, Molly. I'm not."

"There aren't any horses that big. I'm going to saddle up a quarter horse for you to ride and a very gentle one. Then next time you come out you can ride the Dancer."

"Yeah, sure."

Molly showed Danny the tack room and explained all the leads and bits and showed him how Manny shoed the horses. Danny loved Amazing Grace and the palomino took an apple from his hand. Then Danny brushed her with a currycomb. Grace seemed to like him, even licked him across the face with a long darting tongue. She lowered her head so that Danny could scratch around her ears the way Molly showed him and soon the two were friends.

By the time Molly and Danny worked their way to Augie's stall, he was nowhere to be seen. Molly peeked over the half door and motioned for Danny to join her. There, down in the hay, was a stallion in training. Handsome Augie was sound asleep. His lips quivered, his ears twitched and every now and then his legs would move as if he were running in his dream. He was beautiful. His chest eased up and down. Danny turned to see Molly smiling as if Augie was her own little boy.

"I'm sorry," Molly whispered, "but I never wake him. He grows and heals while he sleeps and I never want to wake him until he's ready."

"He's the best," Danny whispered.

"He sure is," Molly said. "Okay. Let's let him do his thing and maybe he'll be up when we get back."

Molly handed Danny a saddle and blanket and took a set of her own. The two went out to the corral to saddle a couple of the remaining quarter horses. Little Bit and Two Bits were brothers and the most quiet, gentle horses on the farm. Molly carried her saddle easily and Danny struggled with his, but soon they made it to the corral. Molly explained how the blanket had to be laid perfectly before cinching down the saddle. She showed Danny how to properly mount his horse—always from the left and always after letting the horse know you were about to get on his back. She explained that horses hate surprises and loud noises and almost anything unexpected, so a horse should be looked at and talked to before being expected to accept a rider. Danny listened carefully and talked gently to Little Bit before Molly helped him get a foot in a stirrup, hold the saddle horn, and then flip his leg over the horse's back. Manny, Marty, Karen, and Rosa pretended not to watch as Molly led the horses out of the corral and into the pasture.

"We don't have any fishing rods," Danny said as now the two horses walked side by side. "Shouldn't we have fishing rods?"

"Nope, gonna catch them with our hands," Molly said, waiting for Danny's reaction. "I'm teasing. The rods are already out there. I just put them in the bulrushes—no sense in bringing them back and forth."

"Won't someone steal them?"

"No, old Scooter would attack them."

"That hundred year old dog on the porch?"

"Don't tell him that. He thinks he's a puppy. I'm teasing about Scooter. He couldn't get out here without having a heart attack. We leave the rods out there because no one steals here. The rods are old, but they work fine. I cover them in plastic and I keep some burlap bags out there that look too shabby for holding oranges. They're just right for fish."

"Think we'll catch any?"

"I can pretty much guarantee it. How you doing with the riding?"

"My butt's a little sore, but this is cool."

"Try to shift your weight as Little Bit walks. You kind of get into a rhythm and you won't be as sore tomorrow. You ready to gallop?"

"Next time," Danny said.

When they reached the pond Molly held a finger to her lips as a reminder to not spook the fish. She tied the horses in the shade of a tree and held Danny's shoulders as he came down off his horse. Quietly, she retrieved two fishing rods and a broom handle with a net attached to one end and then walked with Danny away from the pond.

"Okay, you need to learn about casting," she whispered. "You hold this button down and then, just as you get the rod even with you, let go. I'm going to put a hunk of apple on your hook and you try it. You pull back and then move forward and then let go. Try it."

At first Danny couldn't cast at all and the line tangled near his face and the apple chunk almost hit him in the mouth. By the third cast he was getting the line out in front of him. Finally, by the tenth practice, the line paid out nearly to the top of the hill.

"By golly, city boy," Molly said, smiling with her freckles perfect in the setting sun, "I do believe you've got it."

Molly pulled a nasty looking bucket from under the tree and retrieved two long squiggly night crawlers. Girls were supposed to be afraid of worms, but Molly attached a crawler on each line and motioned for Danny to follow her down the bank.

"See where that stump top is?" she whispered. "Try to cast next to it and as you reel in jerk a little like the worm is hurt."

"Hurt?"

"Yeah, like he's got a problem or something. Just like us, fish want an easy meal. Each time you jerk, wait a few seconds before you start reeling. Trust me. Do it."

"What about you?"

"I can catch them all the time."

Danny cast his line toward the stump and reeled in slowly. Then he let fly again and reeled, looking at Molly who nodded her head that he was doing it exactly right. On Danny's third cast, a huge mouth grabbed the crawler and raced for the middle of the pond.

"Set the hook!" Molly shouted. "Yank him, Dan! Good. Now reel! Come on, Danny Baby—reel!"

Suddenly a bass broke the surface and tail-walked twenty feet away. He was a big one and now he dove to the bottom. Danny could feel the fish jerking to free the hook and again he came out of the water and shook his head. Again the fish took the line and swam back toward the stump.

"Don't let him get you by that stump. He's trying to break you off. Walk down here, Danny. Steady pressure. Good. Pull up and reel your way down. Here he comes. He's a dandy. Keep coming, Dan."

In a second Molly scooped into the water with her net and up came a four-pound bass. Danny had an amazed look on his face and now this incredible girl held up the biggest fish Danny had ever caught. He was excited and Molly kept smiling.

"Hold him," Molly said as Danny held his bass and stared at it. "I brought a camera in my saddle bag and we'll get your picture with him."

"This has been an awesome day. Molly, I never had a better day."

Molly snapped several pictures and explained to Danny it would be better to let the big fish go and catch smaller ones which would taste better. And if this big fish were female, it would be wise to leave her to spawn and stock the pond. The two moved down to the other end of the pond and caught three more bass and two sunfish, all of which Molly put into a burlap bag.

"I guess we'd better get going," Molly said. "Your parents will be coming soon and I want to clean these fish for you."

"Could we sit here on the bank a little longer?" Danny asked.

"Sure, you sit and I'll be right back. I'll put the junk away so we can go in a few minutes."

Danny sat on the bank and watched Molly put away the fishing gear and then he watched her return. She sat next to him and pointed where the moon was just starting to rise. Neither spoke for the longest time and now Danny leaned back on his elbows and looked at the girl who had just shown him a remarkable day.

"See this little freckle right here?" Danny asked, touching the middle of Molly's cheek.

"Of course I can't see it," Molly answered. "Plus, unfortunately, I have hundreds of them. Why did you pick out just one?"

"Your freckles are wonderful, but this one is my favorite. Would it wreck the day if I asked if I could kiss this one freckle?"

"I guess not."

Danny was on his knees and Molly was embarrassed. He seemed to take forever, but then he tenderly kissed Molly's cheek. His lips were so soft and he so barely kissed the surface of her skin, it kind of tickled.

"Wow, Molly let me kiss my favorite freckle."

"Was a certain one really your favorite?"

"It is now," Danny whispered and looked away.

"Thank you."

"No, thank you, Molly. I said once that I met you too early. I knew right away you'd be as great as you are. Now, how am I supposed to hold on to you seven or eight years?"

"What do you mean?"

"I mean you haven't been discovered yet. I won't stand a chance when you are."

"Just be Danny and we'll be fine."

They rode back to the house in silence and every now and then Molly touched her face where Danny's kiss had been and she smiled. Danny was more handsome than some of the boy band members on MTV. He hadn't been discovered either. How was she supposed to compete with the girls with the makeup and designer jeans? She decided to relax and enjoy the moment. The future would take care of itself.

By the time the Freemans arrived in their Lincoln, the fish had been cleaned and Molly added some catfish to the bag and wrote a note about how to cook them. She and Danny sat on the swing and watched the moon rise above the barn. Manny had taken Rosa home and Marty and Karen finished putting away the dishes. Danny watched his parents' car coming up the drive. He touched Molly's hand.

"Molly," Danny said, "it'll take a heck of a day to beat this one. There is no one like you."

"I'm just Molly from the farm."

"You think anyone can beat that?" Danny asked.

Before Molly could answer, the Lincoln stopped in front of Grandpa Grimaldi's magnificent porch.

CHAPTER TWELVE

Moving Day for Manny

There had been tornadoes touching down in West Palm and bad weather was headed for Ocala. It was odd that tornadoes would be possible here at the end of hurricane season. The same swing that Molly and Danny swung on two months ago at the picnic was now unhooked and carted out to the barn. Manny herded the cows into the same corral and the horses were taken to the barn. The weathervane on top on the barn twirled furiously. Marty chased chickens into the hen house. The wind had picked up to fifty or more miles per hour. Dark clouds were coming in from the south.

Inside the house Molly secured and locked the southern windows, then she brought in the lawn furniture from the porch and stacked the chairs on the floor. She ran to both bathrooms and began to run water in the tubs; then she collected matches, candles, flashlights, and lanterns and put them all by the front door. The farmhouse would need water and light sources if they lost power. Molly went to the kitchen and made a double portion of cornbread. She slipped both flat pans into the oven and set the timer. If the power went out in the next few minutes, the cornbread would be slop and she'd throw it out, but if the storm could hold off twenty minutes there would be fresh cornbread to eat while they rode it out. Next, she went into the front room and collected breakables from the fireplace mantel and framed pictures from the tables and placed them all on the floor of a living room closet. If a window shattered as it had two years ago, precious momentos would be safe from the wind. She returned to shut off the bathroom faucets and placed buckets near each bathtub. Then she went back to the kitchen to take out the finished cornbread and put both tins in the sink to cool.

Now Molly went to help her father in the barn. Feverishly they tossed hay into stalls and filled troughs with water. The horses wouldn't eat during the worst of the storm, especially if there was lightning and thunder, but they would be hungry and thirsty eventually and the Grimaldis might not be able to make it out to the barn.

"This storm hits those orange groves and we're in real trouble!" her father shouted. "There's nothing we can do. The horses will be fine and the cows will have to hunker down and ride it out. You see any funnels?"

"There were a few dip-downs to our south, but I couldn't see any rotation. The weather channel said three touchdowns south of here and maybe we're just going to get high winds and no touches."

"That's bad enough. You go into the house and get the sleeping bag out for Manny. I don't want him in that shack. Did you get everything squared away in the house?"

"Everything is fine. You need for me to do anything else?"

By the time Marty put the locking board in place to secure the barn his shirt was flapping like a flag in the wind. Marty and Manuel stood on the porch and watched a dark green-edged cloud move toward the east end of the farm. Lightning zipped and thunder crackled. Then there was a quiet in the air. The rain started with plopping big drops; then almost immediately falling in torrents. Dry when he left the barn, Marty was drenched by the time he made it to the porch. The cloud seemed lower now and dark fingers from it crept downward. Huge thunderclaps resonated and echoed. The wind was up. Molly hugged her father tightly. Suddenly there was a huge blast from the east and Marty knew the transformers had blown. There would be no power.

"There she blows," her father said. "At least we have the generator and that'll give us eight hours or so."

"You want it on now, boss?"

"Not yet, Manny. Let's wait until midnight or so. We can use candles and flashlights until then. There's no telling how many people are without power. It could be a few days. Let's get into the house now. The worst action will be knocking at the door in a few minutes."

Marty was right. He built a huge fire and before the flames could take solid hold the rain began coming in slants and it was as dark as night. Every few seconds bolts of lightning would illuminate the room and, even though she knew they were coming, Molly flinched every time. Poor Augie must be horrified. Molly hoped he was down in his stall with his head buried in the hay. As the storm raged all around, Molly worried the windows would burst. She burrowed down in her chair and watched the fire and tried to take her mind off Augie and the other horses and the cows left out in the rain. There was the sound of wood creaking and cracking and Marty crawled on hands and knees to see if the house had been compromised. He returned from the kitchen saying he found nothing. It was frightening. Day converged with night.

Three hours later the storm was still raging and somehow Molly fell asleep. Occasionally she would bolt awake with new strokes of lightning. Then her eyes would close again. Marty and Manny listened to a transistor radio. Finally the worst of the storm had passed and was headed for the gulf. The newscaster said there were two more touchdowns, but now the storm was labeled a thunder storm. Over fifty thousand homes in the area were without power and several roads were impassible because of flash flooding. The farmhouse had weathered the storm, but something happened in that first hour. Marty prayed it wasn't the barn.

Strangely enough, Molly was first to wake up. Apparently her father and Manny had been up most of the night because she could hear the generator running. She blinked her eyes to get her bearings and she looked across the dim great room to see her father snoring and asleep in his lounge chair and Manny nestled on the floor in his sleeping bag. The rain on the roof lacked the power and authority of last night's storm. She eased off the blanket that someone had covered her with and tiptoed out to the kitchen to make coffee. The pump was running so the generator was working efficiently. There was water at the faucet and electricity. She looked outside. It was a bad vantage point but she could still see the cows had separated and now were milling around the corral. Concerned about how the farm had fared she put on tennis shoes and a slicker and walked out the back door to look.

At the back of the house everything seemed fine. There were tree branches down and the weathervane had blown off the barn. Somehow it ended up here lodged against a split rail fence. The rain was steady now, but the wind had stilled. The air was dank and humid. She went out to the corral and released the cows out into the pasture, all the while she looked at the barn. Thankfully, the barn looked none the worse for wear. If the weathervane was the only damage the storm caused they had been very fortunate. She took the huge wooden crossbar out of the door hinges and walked into to the barn. The horses were very important. She hoped there was no damage to the back of the barn. There had been a sound of wood breaking somewhere near the house. She opened the first barn door and hoped the back of the barn hadn't given in—Augie was at the back of the barn. Maybe she should have waited for Manny and her father in case there was disaster here, but instead she opened the second door and walked inside.

The barn was safe! It was almost as if nothing had been bothered. She took attendance. She would return with fresh water and food. Dancer was up and making his usual racket and when Molly rubbed his nose and kept going he began to kick his stall wall at the fact that this visit was supposed to mean apples. Amazing Grace looked over her half door. She was fine. The quarter horses and the Arabians looked strong and healthy, but Augie was not to be seen. Now Molly walked slowly toward his stall. Usually he could smell her coming and he would be up and excited to see her. There was no sign of him. A hundred thoughts bumped together in her brain. She came close enough to look over the side. Molly held her chest and burst out laughing. There was Augie, almost totally covered with hay, with his lips quivering as he slept. This time Molly would make an exception. She knelt down and kissed his nose until his eyes opened.

"Well, good morning," Molly said. Augie jumped to his feet and licked her all over her face. "Glad to see me?"

Augie seemed to want to tell her all about the storm and he turned his head and made noises Molly had never heard him make before. It was as though he was telling her the whole story of how he had gotten through the night and he didn't want to miss any of the details. Molly laughed and Augie licked and nodded. Her little stallion had made it through his first storm.

Molly looked all around the barn. It seemed totally untouched. This would be great news. Soon she would go in and tell her father and Manny that everything was good. But something had happened during the night, and if it wasn't the house or the barn, what else could it be? She scooped up a box of corn pellets and headed out to the chicken coop. The chickens had been holed up all night and they would be happy to get out even if they had to walk through the slop and rivers of water the storm had caused. She walked around the opposite end of the house, through the chicken wire gate, and opened the door to the coop. Chickens flew out as if the coop were on fire and Molly was coated with feathers all over her face and even inside her raincoat. It took a while for the chickens to see Molly had poured corn pellets in all the steel dishes. Then they swarmed their food.

Molly looked over at Manny's house. "Oh no," she whispered, "oh no."

Manny's little twenty feet by fifteen feet rectangular cabin had lost its roof. The back wall was leaning in, ready to fall. Looking west, Molly saw parts of the roof at least several hundred feet away. Molly walked toward Manny's little cabin. It had once been a cabin for laborers, but Manny took it over and made it into a little home. He had his television, a hot plate, his Spanish books and magazines, his bed, a small bathroom with a shower. That was all he ever wanted. Even though he was regularly invited to sleep in the farmhouse spare bedroom, he always chose to go home to his little house. Molly stepped onto the small wooden porch and wrestled with the now bowed front door. It was horrible. The storm sucked out most of the contents and deposited muck over some heavy objects that were banged around and broken. Manny's house was lost. Manny, who had so little, now had nothing.

Molly touched nothing. She knew the power to Manny's cottage would need to be turned off at the power pole. Manny would have to move into the main house now. Manny loved his privacy. Now the storm took that away too. As she looked around at what was left, Molly began to cry, realizing what could have happened to Manny if he had not spent the night in the big house. But, Manny was alive and well and that was what was important.

Molly headed back to the farmhouse trudging through the mud and little rivers that ran downhill toward the barn. The rain had stopped completely. It didn't matter. Molly's tennis shoes were ruined. That didn't matter either. Molly was bringing a wonderful friend terrible news. At the door, she shook off her raincoat. She could hear her father and Manny talking in the kitchen. Molly entered the kitchen and hugged her father. Manny jumped up to pour her a cup of coffee.

"Get those socks off and throw them in the garbage," her father said. "How'd you get up so early?"

"I wanted to go out and see what the storm did."

"How did we do? The horses and cows okay?"

"They're fine," Molly mumbled. "I put the cows out, fed the chickens, and checked out the horses. All our living things are fine." Her lip trembled.

"What isn't fine, Molly? I know you. What's wrong?" her father asked.

"Manny," Molly started, ignoring her father, "I'm going to say this right out. The wood cracking in the storm was the roof of your cabin."

"What did you see?" Manny asked.

"The roof of the cabin is gone. Inside everything is ruined. I'm so sorry." Tears streamed down her cheeks.

Molly hugged Manny hard, but he seemed to be staring into space. Slowly he sat down at the table and sipped his coffee. His eyes locked onto Molly's eyes.

"My books? My pictures? My records?"

"I don't know, Manny. Everything looks like a wet mess. I hope some of your things are still there, dry under the muck."

"We will have breakfast," Manny was strangely calm. "Then we will go look at my home. Your father cooked some sausages and you could make up some eggs. The coffee was very good this morning."

"Manny, I love you and I'm sorry."

"We will have breakfast," Manny said. "We need to see the whole farm and the groves and we should eat first. I am pleased the buildings and the critters are okay. Nothing else happened?"

"The weathervane is down. Some limbs got knocked off the big tree. The hay in the corral is blown all over. Some little things have been blown around."

"That's good," Manny said. "This is a good farm and it must always survive. You got a bed for me, boss? I could bed in the barn for a while."

"You will live in the house until you don't need to."

Marty said nothing else and stabbed at his sausages and finished his coffee before slamming down his empty cup. He was angry. His dark brown eyes stared straight ahead. The three sat and ate in silence until Manny took his plate to the sink. Breakfast was over.

The men waited while Molly put on new socks and rubber boots. Then the group headed for what was left of Manny's cabin. Marty stopped at the power pole and pulled out two main fuses from the junction box. Manny walked ahead of Molly. Still twenty feet away, he stood rooted to one spot and took in the destruction that was his home. He raised his hands over his head, then lowered his arms and interlaced his fingers around the back of his neck and rocked back and forth. Molly and her father stood back while Manny went toward his front door. He disappeared inside. Soon he was crying and shouting in Spanish. Molly moved to join Manny but Marty held her arm.

"Let him have this time and his space."

"Don't you think that's a little mean?"

"No," Marty said flatly, "do as I say."

After ten minutes Manny emerged with a box of phonograph records. He sat on the porch and hugged the records to him as one would a child. His black hair hung in ringlets over his forehead. Marty nudged his daughter forward and motioned for her to sit with Manny while he had a look inside at the remains of the house. Molly sat next to Manny. When she put her arm around him, his shoulders suddenly seemed so small.

He said nothing. Every so often he pulled up his shirt end to dab it at his eyes. He shivered. Molly wondered if she should call Rosa.

Marty came out of the cabin with fire in his eyes. He walked toward the van they used for street travel.

"Where are you going, Dad?"

"I'll be back directly," he answered without turning around.

After a while Manny rose to his feet. He took his box and started walking toward the house. At least he spoke to tell Molly where he was going.

"There's nothing to do here, little girl." Great sadness was in his eyes. "I'll go check the groves. There's nothing more to be done here."

"Manny?"

"Everything will be fine. You tell boss where I went when he comes back."

Manny took off in the jeep. Normally he would saddle a horse and enjoy the morning sun. Now he bounced down the road and turned off in the pasture, scattering the cows as he headed toward the seedlings.

Molly fed the horses. Now they were calm. She thought how men acted so strangely in the face of tragedy. Marty actually said nothing to Manny. He just jumped in the van and drove away. Sure, he was angry, but shouldn't he have stayed around to offer help to Manny?

"I got plans for you, Dancer," she said. "Did you slink down for the storm or were you ready to fight with it? You're such a tough guy. You think you can even beat Grace in the half mile? I'm thinking you got slow. You're just all washed up, huh?"

Molly moved to Augie taking him out to the small corral for exercise and to let him see her ride off on Grace. Molly trotted Grace to the farmhouse, stopped to pick up a heavy duty black garbage bag, then trotted her out to what was left of Manny's cabin. She circled it, then headed in a straight line due west until she saw shingles and boards scattered several feet apart. Here she jumped off Grace's back in a bound and landed perfectly on her feet. The mare followed and Molly walked. Soon Molly bent down and picked up a book. It was Manny's. When the storm sucked off the roof and almost everything in the cabin, Manny's things had to go somewhere. Now Molly saw two more books, both in Spanish, but both in better shape than the first. She put the treasures in a bag usually meant for garbage and she continued to walk. Ahead was Manny's toaster. It had a huge dent in the side. Molly tossed it into her bag. Next she found a cane, a cowboy hat, and, separated by fifty feet, Manny's fancy riding boots that he wore Sundays and other special times. She tied the bag onto the saddle horn and led Grace to a small grove of wild palms. The thickets around the palms could have caught things blowing through during the high winds. Sure enough, here she found the treasure of treasures. Molly brushed off the cover of Manny's photo album. Luckily the album's leather strap and snap kept it closed. It must have tumbled end over end until coming to rest. Molly held her breath and unsnapped the strap. Every picture was safe. She continued searching and found Manny's jockey shirt, a rain soaked picture of himself and Rosa at the barbecue, and a trophy Manny won during his riding days. Molly and Grace ranged over a hundred feet or so and she and found some more pictures, a hairbrush, a pair of jeans, and an embroidered shirt. They were filthy and the pictures were stained, but nonetheless treasures.

Molly put the plastic bag in her room and came back out to take off Grace's saddle and let her walk out in the pasture. She brought some apples for Augie to fetch and eat. She tossed each one in a different direction and carefully watched her foal's legs as he raced to get them. It felt strange that Manny was riding fence and Marty had disappeared. Right this second she was in control of the entire farm. Right now she was boss. She looked all around 3-M Farm and knew it was the one place she could never leave. The house was the work of her forefathers and the barn had been constructed by precious friends. She was connected to this place. She would find a way to stay here all of her life.

An hour later Marty returned in a totally different mood. He jumped out of the van and ran into the house to call Karen. He waved at Molly. His smile had returned. Whatever he had done mysteriously changed him and now he sat on the swing talking on the phone with Karen. He was smoking his pipe—something he never did in the middle of the day. Marty was a curious man. In the face of Manny's hurt he was happy. Molly waited for him to get off the phone. He sure looked younger than he had this morning.

Ready to talk to her, Marty asked, "Where's Manny? Where is the old boy?"

"What the heck are you so happy about? Maybe we should blow up the barn and then you can be in a great mood."

"You'll see. Where's Manny?"

"You answer my question and I'll answer yours."

"No, really," her father said, his face beaming. "Where is Manny?"

"Dad, what's wrong with you? He's out checking the orange groves and his gardens. I don't think he'll appreciate your attitude."

"You don't, huh? I think if he has a glass of lemonade everything will be fine."

"What?"

"Life gives you lemons—you make lemonade."

"Are you going to tell me what's going on?"

"Nope, but you'll see."

"Does Karen know?"

"Yep, Karen knows, but you'll find out soon."

"You think you can wipe the smile off your face when Manny returns?"

"I doubt it."

"You need to wear a hat in the sun, Dad."

"Yep, you're right. Maybe I'm going to buy myself a brand new hat. What do you think of that? I might buy a twenty-gallon hat with spangles and rhinestones all over it. Treat me right and I'll buy one for you too."

"As if I would wear it. You're losing it, Dad."

"Nope, I'm finding it. Well, I've got chores to do." Molly worried that her father had lost his mind.

At lunch Manny reported the storm must have touched down beyond the seedlings. They were fine, the orchards were fine and the vegetables were beaten up but looked like they would make a comeback. The whole time Marty Grimaldi was beaming. It was a ridiculous situation.

The answer to Marty Grimaldi's new mood came early the next morning. There was a huge noise down the road, but her father insisted everyone sit tight and enjoy breakfast. Once Molly got up to go look out the window, but Marty pointed her back to her chair. Manny's head was down bowed over his plate. He was very sad. Marty hand-signalled Molly that he would look out the window. He turned around, rubbed his hands together, and rumbled Manny's hair. Manny said nothing. A few minutes later Marty went out on the porch and met a mysterious man, and signed official papers the man held out.

"The farmer said to the boll weevil," Marty sang, returning to the table. "Say, why did you pick my farm?"

"What is wrong with you?" Molly was begging her father for an answer to his strange behavior. Manny glared straight ahead.

"Boll weevil said to the farmer," Marty continued. "Ain't gonna do you much harm—just looking a home."

"Boss," Manny started, his tone showed his annoyance with Captain Happy.

"Come on, you two," Marty said, putting his hands up to protect himself. "Before you hit me, let's go for a walk."

"I'm not sure I want to go anywhere with you," Molly said. She and Manny got up and walked to the door.

In a place a hundred feet closer to the road than the barn, Marty pointed to a gigantic mobile home. It was twice the size of Manny's cabin and, while it wasn't sparkling new, it was beautiful.

"What?" Manny asked. He seemed stunned.

"All hooked up and ready to go, my friend," Marty said with a huge smile. "Two bedrooms in case you and Rosa want children. I got a great deal from that park that sold to developers and, my wonderful friend, it's all yours."

"Martin?" Manny asked, "can this be mine?"

"All yours. You ever leave; you take your house with you."

"I never had a house," Manny said.

"You have one now. Go take a look while I talk to my little girl. Go on. We'll have to buy some second hand things and some things I know I can't replace. Go check it out, Manny."

"Boss, I can't."

"Go on now before we waste the whole day."

Molly and Marty watched Manny walk to his new home. This time he raised his hands over his head in happiness and shouted, "gracias!" again and again as he discovered the amenities of his home.

"Dad," Molly asked, "can we afford this?"

"We can't afford not to do this. I always hated him living in that little house. Manny is a man. We're nothing without Manny. He is my friend and my brother."

"But can we afford this?"

"I had a little insurance on his place and then we used a little of the emergency fund. I reckon that Manny being happy and satisfied at all times is an emergency."

"Dad, I love you very much."

"I love you, too, Molly. Love is action instead of words. Your actions, and Manny's let me know how very fortunate I am."

At dinner Manny was the most talkative Molly had ever heard him. He went on and on about his new home and told them all about the things they had already seen. "I'll have to sleep in the big house a few more nights until I get furniture, but now I can start planning with Rosa and really think about children." The whole time, Marty smiled.

"I have to go get dessert, Manny," Molly said, winking at her father. "I'm keeping dessert in my room."

A minute later Molly Grimaldi returned with the black garbage bag and handed it to Manny. He looked confused, so Molly motioned for him to turn the bag around and pour its contents out on the floor. In a flash, out came a bruised toaster, the boots, pictures, Manny's beloved books, the embroidered shirt, and, finally, the family photo album Manny was sure had been lost in the storm. Manny's eyes were wide and he was smiling.

CHAPTER THIRTEEN

Living in Different Centuries

Danny visited the farm a second time. He had a job to do. Although his romance with Molly had been steady, Danny never asked for more than his one freckle kiss. Every now and then he would touch his favorite freckle and smile his huge smile. Molly was perfectly comfortable that they were friends beyond anything else. Every now and then they would hold hands on the bus. There seemed a mutual understanding that the more slowly they went the longer the relationship would last. They talked on the phone on occasion. This time Molly called Dan.

"I need some help on a little project I'm working on," she said into the phone. "You think you could come over for a couple of hours?"

"Sure, my mom and sister are going to the mall in Ocala and I don't want to go. They could drop me off and pick me up on the way home."

"Perfect."

By the time Danny arrived Molly had already saddled Amazing Grace and had her waiting in the small corral. Molly made sure she spoke with Mrs. Freeman and Danny's sister Andrea and soon they left for a shopping adventure. It was no wonder Danny didn't want to go. Mrs. Freeman remembered how everyone but Andrea loved the catfish Molly sent a couple months back and she invited Molly to come swim in the backyard pool. Molly agreed, but she doubted she would go. Molly didn't own a bathing suit because she'd never learned to swim. The few times she had been to the ocean, she'd gone in only up to her knees, rolling up her jeans. She mused that busy farm girls usually did not do much swimming.

142

"So, what do you need me to do?" Danny asked.

"Okay," Molly said. "This is the deal. Let's get Augie into the small corral. See the bigger corral? If you measure it close to the split rail, it's exactly two furlongs."

"What?"

"It's two furlongs."

"What is a furlong?"

"Oh yeah—a furlong is a little over two hundred yards. The important part is that a furlong is about one eighth of a mile."

"Why is that important?"

"Races are determined by the number of furlongs. If a horse ran around this track six times that would be the distance of most major races."

"Six times?"

"Yep, people don't realize how far and how fast race horses have to run. Here, take this whistle. What I want to teach Augie is how to run a circular pattern rather than just willy-nilly all around the track. I'm going to run ahead of him with Grace and see if he follows. Augie's never run full out and it's time to see what he has."

"What's the whistle for?"

"I'll be on Grace's back and looking ahead. There will be times I won't be able to see Augie. If he stumbles, the least little bit, you blow that whistle like a madman. I'll stop and he'll stop. If he falls to the ground, you blow the whistle and then run to the house and call Karen Cable. She's the vet."

"Should we be doing this?"

"Augie's six months old and he needs to run. I can't baby him all his life or he won't have the one he is meant to. I've watched him in the little corral. He's undisciplined, but he's fast."

"Do you want him to be a race horse?"

"That's the general idea. Now, do you know what to do?"

"Yeah, you're going to run ahead and if Augie has problems I blow the whistle?"

"And what else?"

"If he falls, I call the vet and get your dad."

Molly took Grace out to the big corral and her foal followed like a puppy. Every time he almost caught up with Molly and Grace, Molly would nudge Grace's flanks and pick up the pace. For the first two furlongs, once around the track, Molly worked up to a slow trot and Augie loped along behind. He seemed happy to be running an unbroken distance. Now Molly moved to a canter. Danny Augie run effortlessly. Danny also watched Molly's ponytail dancing in the wind and now she leaned close to Grace's neck. Augie lagged behind them. Molly turned around and shouted Augie's name. As if he shifted gears, Augie's legs extended. He ran and closed the distance. Danny was amazed a little horse could run so fast. Soon Augie was hugging the rail and running full out. Molly kicked Grace's sides gently, and now the palomino was a full gallop. Only a few yards behind, Augie's legs didn't seem to touch the ground as he ran with his head down and ears back. He was as fast as lightning. He was keeping pace with a full-grown adult horse. Grace wasn't racetrack fast but she was fast enough. Molly smiled broadly, slowed and let Augie get even with Grace. Then she shouted, "Augie, Whoa!"

They walked the last furlong to let the horses cool down. Grace was tired, but Augie pranced next to her as if he wanted to play the running game a while longer. Danny had never blown the whistle and Augie walked evenly now. Danny came out on the track and intercepted Augie and praised him.

"Did you see that?" Molly shouted, jumping off Grace and letting her walk alone. "Augie, you ran like a scalded dog. You liked it, too, didn't you? Augie, you ever heard of a horse called Funny Cide?"

"Is he really that fast?" Danny asked.

"With no one on his back, he's very fast. I've seen colts six months older than Augie. They're not as fast as he is. He's a year away from a rider, but he's quick all right."

"So, someday you'll race him?"

"I've got someone else on my mind right now, but I think I have to train him as if he might race. Today was very good. I didn't know if he would run. He might have just stood still. Boy, did you see him gear up when I called his name?"

"Sure did. He really poured it on."

"Yeah, but that's not the good thing. Manny says a good racehorse has to have what's called 'second speed.' What that means is that they can be called on to run faster. If a horse can be talked into moving up a notch, he'll stretch out to the max. Seabiscuit and Secretariat had that. They would be running full out and their jockeys could ask them to find a new gear. That's second speed. I think Augie may have it."

Augie seemed barely winded. He was still excited. Augie showed he would run fast. Molly told Danny that for a horse to run head down and ears back showed focus and determination.

"Danny," Molly said, "at one point when Augie closed the distance between himself and Grace he was actually running faster than his mother.

"You're really a good rider," Danny said. "I couldn't believe how fast you were going on that second lap. I could never learn to do that."

"I've been riding since I was a kid. We had an old chestnut my father and mother let me ride when I was five. They called him 'Murphy.' He had only one speed: slow. Murphy was the gentlest horse in the world and I don't think I ever saw him run. Even when it stormed and the horses hurried back to go in the barn, about a half hour later Murphy would wander back from the pasture. My dad said Murph probably didn't know it was raining. He wasn't that old. He just took his time doing everything. My mom would put me on Murphy's back at the porch and it would take him ten minutes to stroll to the barn and back. I graduated from Murphy to other horses. I'm not great at riding a bike, but I can ride a horse."

"What ever happened to Murphy?"

"My mom sold him to a circus that came through Ocala. We hated to see Murph go, but the man who bought him was a photographer who took pictures of children on Murphy's back. Now Murph has seen more of the country than I have. My mom checked out the whole situation and Murphy inherited a pretty good deal. The photographer's horse died after about thirty years. He had to get a new horse or he had no job with the circus. Murphy was so gentle he was perfect. Other than being my first riding horse, Murph didn't pull his weight here. He wouldn't pull anything and there was no way he could herd cattle. The average cow was faster than Murph. I miss him. He had lots of personality."

"Isn't one horse about the same as the next?"

"That might be true of lawnmowers, but I doubt even that. Every horse is totally different from the next. Some are very smart and teachable. Others are lazy and stubborn. Some will work all day and others will bolt for the barn. They're just like people. In Murphy's case, he was way out there. I think he was a little slow witted. He even ate slowly. If another horse pushed him off his hay, he'd just wander away. There would be more hay tomorrow. He was just totally content with his lot in life. Maybe all the activity of a circus sparked him up a little, but I doubt it. Murphy was Murphy."

"So, when will Augie be able to have a rider?"

"In about a year. I want to have him run with blankets on his back and then I'll saddle him and let him get used to that weight. Have you ever seen a sway back horse?"

"The kind where their backs slope way back like the middle of a slinky?"

"Exactly. Someone rode them too early. I'll let Augie accept a rider at eighteen months, but just for short distances. It'll help him build his back muscles. I won't rush him."

"You want him to race?"

"If he has the temperament for it. You saw today he likes to run with another horse and that's a good sign."

"Isn't that mean horse a racehorse?"

"Dancer isn't mean. He's just arrogant. He's a stallion and he thinks he's all that. He used to be a race horse, but he isn't much of one now."

"Why? Did he get slower or something?"

"He might be faster than ever. Today was not about getting Augie to be a race horse. Today was about getting Dancer to be a race horse again."

"I don't get it."

"I won't explain it right now, but you might have helped Dancer become the horse he was. I'm working on an idea that I haven't even shared with my father yet."

"You still haven't explained why Dancer can't race anymore."

"Because he would lose. He got his spirit broken and probably Grace would beat him now. Remember Augie's burst of speed? Dancer does the opposite and pulls up when another horse closes in on him. It's a long story, but speed is just as much in the head as it is the legs."

"What does Augie have to do with it?"

"Everything," Molly said, without further explanation. "What are you doing for Christmas?"

"I think we're going to Baltimore," Danny said. "I really would have preferred to stay here. I could have gotten to see you and go fishing and riding, but we have friends and a few family members in Maryland and my dad says we're going there. How about you?"

"We'll stay here. We always do. Karen and Rosa will come out and Manny wants to have Christmas in his new mobile home. I'm guessing it'll all be Mexican food."

"That sounds great."

"I'm looking forward to it. In fact, when I get older every Christmas dinner I make will be foods from a different country. Some turkeys might be happy about that."

"I like that idea."

Molly and Danny hung out for most of the afternoon, doing chores. He fed chickens. He cleaned the stalls. He pet and fed horses. Still he came nowhere near Dancer's stall. He helped clean manure and put it in barrels so Manny could make his secret mixture to fertilize his gardens. He pulled weeds from the vegetable patch. Finally, he went with Molly to the house for lunch.

"You still want to be a farmer, young man?" Marty asked. "I saw you working hard out there."

"I don't know, Mr. Grimaldi. Already, every muscle I have is sore. Farming looks neat from a distance. Up close, it's back breaking work."

"Oh," Marty said. "You learn to love it."

"I need to get in shape. Molly's twice as strong as I am. I think I might need to go into training."

"There you go, Dad," Molly said. "We could start a shape up farm for city folks. They lose weight and get stronger and we get the chores done and make them pay us. What do you think?"

"You may have something there. Back in farm time Americans ate a huge breakfast as body fuel to work all day. Then, by the time they got back to the house for dinner, they were very hungry. Americans still eat like farmers, but they don't burn off the fuel. They just keep adding more. Now, look at Manny here. He's a lean mean machine. Look at this boy. If he took his shirt off, you'd really see muscle definition."

"Stop teasing, boss." Manny said. "I got the pot stomach because I watch television late at night and eat American— potato chips, soda, and those pizza rolls. You and Molly go to sleep early. That's why you stay thin."

"Don't let him fool you," Marty said. "Manny is strong as a horse. Molly too. You don't get muscles with your hands at your sides, and you saw today you never stop working on a farm. Still interested?"

"You know what?" Danny Freeman said, tossing down the last of a huge hamburger, "Yeah, I like this. I could get stronger and learn to love the land. It sure sounds better than being in an office and wearing a suit and tie. I'll have to get back to you on the part where you shovel the manure."

Marty and Molly drove Danny home to a beautiful neighborhood of manicured lawns and backyard screened-in pools. There were fine cars on most of the circular driveways lined with miniature palm trees. Most of the homes were bi-level. Some of them looked large enough to house ten or fifteen people instead of four or five.. Young adults zoomed around in little decorated golf carts and older people walked poodles and miniature schnauzers down the street. Even though 3-M Farm and Danny's neighborhood were less than three miles apart, they may as well have been in different countries. Molly and Danny seemed to have so much in common, but it was clear they lived in different worlds.

"Would you like to live here?" Marty asked Molly as Danny ran to open his home's elaborate front door. "Pretty fancy smancy stuff here."

"Too much concrete," Molly said. "I mean, it's nice and all that, but there's no dirt here, Dad. Even the places around the trees are covered with bark chips or stones or something. I don't think I would like it much."

"All your chores would be taken care of. You could hire a maid for the dishes and look out the window and watch the maintenance men cut the lawn."

"I'd wonder what to do all day. What do you think they do?"

"I imagine they play golf and join clubs and watch television."

"I'd rather hang out with horses than most people and I can already watch television—maybe not so many channels, but since there's nothing good on the channels we have, why would I want more? As far as golf is concerned, I'm sure it's fun but I don't get it. Isn't the idea of most sports to get the ball? In golf, you already have the ball and then hit it away from yourself. I just feel like people are killing time because they have nothing else to do. We have plenty to do."

"Yeah, but if you marry Danny, you'll need to get some evening gowns and a little tennis outfit and one of those cute golfing outfits so you and Daphne can go out on the links."

"Oh stop it," Molly said. "I doubt Danny and I are getting married any time soon, but if we do he'll get measured for some cowboy boots and I'll hope he doesn't look silly in a hat just like Doc's."

"His parents will be horrified."

"They probably are already horrified. His sister looks at me like I'm Annie Oakley from the Wild West Show."

"That bother you?"

"I am who I am."

"You sure are. Let's go get some staples in town. We need sugar and flour. I'd like to get a bushel of apples. Then I'll reach way down in these jeans to see if there's enough money for a couple of those big ice cream cones."

"Sounds good to me."

Back at the farm Molly finished homework and then went out to throw apples to Augie. She stopped in the barn to let Augie and the Dancer smell each other and snort. Dancer knew there was a connection between himself and this jet-black youngster, but he let Augie know not to get too close. Once Augie was down for the night, Molly went to see Dancer and feed him a couple apples. Of all adult horses she had ever seen, Molly determined there has never been another stallion quite like Dancer. He was all muscle and power and her father had turned down offers into the thousands for him. If something good didn't happen and soon, one day her father would accept one of the offers. With the destruction of one of the orange groves and the money put into Manny's new house, it was quietly understood that 3-M Farm was hanging on by a spider thread.

"Mr. Dancer," Molly said to the giant stallion. "My name is Molly and I am a psychiatrist. Tomorrow you're going in for counseling and I want you to pay close attention. Yep, you have an appointment and I'll be sure you aren't late."

The next morning Molly took Dancer out to the smaller corral and tied him off in the shade. She went back to the barn and first returned with Augie. Then she returned with Grace all saddled and ready to ride. With Dancer wide-eyed and watching, Molly repeated the same thing she had done yesterday. Dancer stared as she and Grace barreled past with Augie in hot pursuit. She stopped long enough to allow the three horses to sniff at one another and then she darted off again. This time she allowed Augie to catch up at the very last moment. Dancer watched his son and nodded his approval. She removed Grace's saddle and let the mare and Augie walk off their exercise. Now Molly walked over to speak to Dancer.

"Okay, big boy, that's it for today. Did you learn anything?"

Every Saturday and Sunday through Christmas and beyond, Molly practiced the same drill. She wouldn't let Dancer run. He was only a spectator but he intently watched every race. Augie was becoming faster. Grace strained to beat her son to the finish. Manny and Marty began taking interest in the weekly races and they marveled at how much Augie seemed to understand. It was not enough to simply run. Almost any horse can run. Augie seemed to understand clearly the goal is to get to the finish line first. By March the mother/son races were thunderous events. Three days before his first birthday, Augie streaked past Grace several yards from the finish line.

True enough, Augie was running without a rider and Grace wasn't exactly a racehorse, but the fact remained that Augie was learning the joy of winning. Soon there was no stopping him. He ran full out from the sound of the bell to the finish line. It became typical for him to beat Grace across the line by seven or eight lengths. Grace didn't seem to want to race any more and would try to pull back toward the barn.

Dancer was placed to watch every race. He nodded and snorted each time his son raced past him. Augie was becoming a little arrogant on his own and he took the opportunity to push at his father's face and snort and puff just like a stallion. Now each time he won a race he pranced and posed in front of Dancer. The older stallion studied Augie with cold and dark eyes.

"You're getting ready to race him, aren't you?" Manny asked one day.

"Who?"

"Stop it. You know I mean Augie."

"I'm not sure I want Augie to race," Molly said mysteriously, and led her colt back to the barn.

"What do you make of that?" Manny asked Marty.

"She's up to something," Marty answered. "Yeah, she's up to something."

CHAPTER FOURTEEN

The Dancer Returns

"Manny, I truly need your help with something very important."

"I would do almost anything for you, Molly."

"I want you to saddle up the Dancer."

"For what purpose?"

"I want to race him."

"You're going to try to race Dancer?"

"You know I can't, but you can."

"You're not about to race your colt against him."

"No, I want you to ride Dancer and Dad to ride Grace."

"This is not a good idea, Molly. Dancer will lose every time. He's twice as fast, but he will lose. He thinks he's supposed to lose. His spirit is already broken. We're out of the racing business."

"I know what you think, but how can Dancer run if he doesn't practice? He only runs hard when you ride him. Even in the pasture, when the other horses run, he stops. I just ask you to do this for me. Once a week I want Dancer and Grace to race."

"This is very bad, but I will do it. Don't you know that Dancer has pride? He will not change his spirit and you will break his heart. Your father and I had him out a week ago and he let a quarter horse pass him. He is broken, Molly. I have seen this before."

Augie was tied off at the big Ficus tree and he tilted his head as he watched his parents being led out from the barn.

Manny rode Dancer and Marty was astride Amazing Grace. Dancer was easily four hands higher and seemed three feet longer than Grace, but he hung his massive head as he and his mate walked side by side into the larger corral. Molly was excited. She waited for the horses to even up and stand still and then she banged a hammer on the bell. On the surface it appeared a total mismatch. While Grace was blond and beautiful, she looked tiny and fragile next to Dancer. Strangely, the moment Dancer heard the bell he broke into a half-hearted gallop but it was obvious he was content to run at Grace's flank. Even when Manny used the crop on the stallion's hindquarters, he would not pass. Furlong after furlong Grace ran full out and Dancer loped along behind her. If he turned on his afterburners, even for a few seconds, Grace would never catch him, but he ran three-quarter speed and stayed in his place. Even after the horses and riders rested and had a second race, the result was the same. Even Augie looked confused and turned his head as his father passed him on his way back to the barn.

Dashaway Dancer was a beaten horse.

"I'm satisfied until next week."

"I don't want to do this again. Dancer has no spirit, but he still has pride. You rub his face in dirt in front of his son."

"I know that's what you think, Manny. Please, just trust me."

"I do what you say," Manny said between clenched teeth. "He is my friend but you make him a fool."

"Molly," her father said as Manny stomped off to the barn. "You hear Manny in the barn yelling in Spanish? I think it's good we don't know what he's saying. You need to give this up. It's no good for Dancer, and it sure isn't helping Manny. He loves that horse."

Molly did not give up. Every Saturday Dancer suffered the humiliation of losing to Grace. All week long Manny was nice enough, but as Saturday approached his attitude toward Molly became chilly and dark. He would saddle the Dancer and rub and kiss at the stallion's muzzle and try to convince he had no real part in all of this. Molly knew the time had come.

"I don't want you to saddle Grace," she said to her father out in the barn.

"Finally come to your senses?" her father answered, "You see the Dancer is done?"

"I'll let you know within the next hour," Molly answered. "Now, do me a favor and tie Grace off by the tree."

"What?"

"I'll be right out."

A few minutes later Manny and Marty talked over the split rail fence and Manny was the first to see what was happening. He tapped Marty. Now both men saw what Molly's plan had been about all along. Molly led Augie from the barn to the big corral and now father and son were on the same side of the fence.

"Whoa, what's going on here, Molly?" her father asked.

"You and I and Grace are going to watch a race."

"Whoa, baby girl. This is a very bad idea."

"Why? You know Augie is fast and he's not afraid."

"I surely don't like this!" Manny shouted. "You make a fool of the Dancer. You will allow his own son to beat him?"

"I'll allow it, but do you think he will?"

"I won't do this."

"Wait a second, Manny," Marty said. "Don't you see Molly's been setting this up all along? First Dancer watches, then

Augie watches, and now Grace watches. You have to admit it is interesting."

"It is cruel."

"It's psychology, Manny," Marty said. "This has never been about Augie. It's been about Dancer from the very beginning. Am I right, Molly?"

"Yes."

"Oh yeah, we're going to do this, Manny. It'll answer the question for all time. I remember my father would let my mother win at checkers from time to time, but he never let me win. Is that what you were thinking, Molly?"

"I guess I was thinking that your father might have let you win if your mother wasn't watching."

"I get it now. Oh yeah, we're doing this," Marty said and he led Augie to the start line. "Molly, you let them quiet down, then ring the bell."

Both Manny and Dancer were very angry. This was an embarrassment to a wonderful horse. Augie knew there was going to be a race and he wrestled Marty for his reins until Marty tied the leads off behind the colt's head. Augie was skittish, but the moment he steadied, Molly rang the bell. Augie shot out before Dancer's first step and now Manny and the stallion gave chase. Marty and Molly held hands as Augie dashed in front of his father and Manny leaned close to Dancer's ears and began shouting in Spanish. After two furlongs Dancer's strides became fluid and strong and Amazing Grace watched as Manny became a jockey and flailed the crop behind him. Suddenly Dancer was right at Augie's flank. Marty and Molly shouted and Grace reared up to break free from her tie to join them at the fence. Augie seemed to slow in mid stride. His legs were still churning but a dark figure next to him suddenly was supercharged. Dancer zoomed past as if his colt were standing still.

"Come on, baby," Molly whispered, but Dancer needed no encouragement. A real thoroughbred again, Dashaway Dancer surged by Augie with his tail full out behind him and Manny hanging on for dear life. Dancer's nostrils flared and his eyes were narrow and focused and clods of dirt and clay flew everywhere. Soon Dashaway Dancer passed his son a second time as if he were saying, "Not today, Junior. Your dad will be in charge this day!" Dancer must have been very close to forty miles per hour when Manny jerked the reins to slow him. Dancer fought the bit and ran harder. Manny pulled a second time and finally Dancer cruised to a trot. He walked over to his tired son, snorted loudly in Augie's face, and pranced so Grace could see him.

"There you go!" Molly shouted. "There you go!"

"I believe we have ourselves a racehorse!" Marty Grimaldi shouted back.

Still Dancer pranced and preened. He held his head high and he was doing an arrogant shuffle that made it seem like he was going sideways. Manny got off Dancer's back and Dancer puffed and walked away from all of them as if they were not worthy of his company. Molly collected her little colt and put him in the small corral with Grace.

"It's okay, baby," she said to her colt. "I'm sorry I set you up. I did what I had to do."

"Molly," Manny asked, "this is what you were doing? You were doing this all for him. You were right. He wasn't going to let his little boy beat him. I love you. I think you just saved a stallion."

"And maybe a farm," Marty added.

CHAPTER FIFTEEN

Love and Marriage on 3-M Farm

Molly's experiment generated spectacular results. Dancer was again bright-eyed, lively, and spirited. He reaffirmed his dominance in the stable, in the barn, and out in the meadow. He charged other male horses and the moment even a small group began to run Dancer would outdistance them and turn around and stare them down. Manny raced Dancer against Grace a couple times and Dancer would bolt at the sound of the bell and leave Grace far behind. It was clear Amazing Grace didn't like all the racing and she seemed relieved when Manny and Marty would saddle other horses to run against Dancer and he easily outran each one. Dancer the racehorse was definitely back. Manny trained him every day. Dancer was his old brash and cantankerous self. There was no meaningful competition left on 3-M Farm so Marty entered the stallion in a two thousand dollar qualifying race at Calder Race Track in Miami.

Marty had to borrow a horse trailer from Mr. Stuart. He and Manny drove in the van. Molly, Karen, and Rosa drove behind in Karen's Bronco. Calder Race Track had newfound popularity since Hialeah had closed and thoroughbreds attracted the largest crowds. Manny had lost ten pounds and looked lean, but he was still one of the older jockeys. The 3-M family looked oddly out of place among the people and horses who competed every week.

Calder's paddocks were crowded with stallions. Several looked as big and strong as Dancer. Dancer had seen this kind of setting before and was not fazed by it. He tried to bite the ear of a big gray that came too close. When Dancer was ready to run he didn't like other horses close to him. He was focused. Only Manny, dressed in blue and white silks, could control him. He reared as the horses for the fourth race were tested for drugs, listed, and lined up. Karen, Molly, and Rosa were in the stands. Marty watched from the paddocks.

"Look," Molly said from her seat in the first row of the grandstand. "Dancer's listed in the program. See: Dashaway Dancer. He's number five."

"Oh, wow," Karen answered. "Look at the odds."

"He's ten-to-one. That's bad, huh Karen?"

"Molly, the odds will change as we get to race time. In fact, his odds will probably get worse. It's his first race at this track and he hasn't raced in nearly two years. Also, we can't forget his reputation as a quitter. Remember he was ahead in his last five races and finished out of the money in all of them."

"Out of the money?" Rosa asked.

"He has to finish in the first three places to win any money at all and there are twelve horses in this race."

"But they don't know how fast he is," Molly said.

"Exactly, but we don't know how fast the other horses are. Don't expect much today. This is a tune-up. We're just trying to see if he'll run at all. I know your dad expects him to be out of the money. He hasn't raced against a field like this in a very long time. You have to remember beating Grace and Augie isn't exactly like running against eleven other thoroughbreds."

"I think we should bet on him," Rosa said. "We know he can run."

"You're the jockey's girlfriend. Betting on him might not be appropriate," Karen said. "I think we should just enjoy the experience and not expect too much. Dancer is out of practice and this is a full mile and a quarter. Even if he finishes in the middle of the pack, we will have had a good day. We just want him to qualify to run again. If he comes in anywhere around two minutes he'll be able to run at this and other tracks. Let's go right down to the finish line. Look, they're bringing out the horses."

"Bet on number five," Rosa whispered to a black woman who disappeared for the betting window. "Manny will win this race. You watch and you will see."

The three women walked to the fence by the finish line and now huge horses passed with tiny men on their backs. Rosa called out to Manny but he kept his eyes straight ahead and pretended not to hear. Molly loved all the hubbub and colors, but she noticed Dancer's saddle looked old and Manny's silk shirt looked faded and wrinkled. The track was beveled and lower at the rail than it was at the outside. The dirt track looked a foot deep. The track at the ranch was flat and the ground was just dirt. The other horses looked more comfortable and confident. Number five acted nervous and skittish. *Karen was probably correct*, Molly thought as she saw Dancer's odds fall to fifteen-to-one. Down to the left, a starting gate was swung into place and a car raced down the track in front of the horses. There was no starting gate at 3-M. Molly knew Dancer wouldn't like being crowded next to other horses, but he moved into his slot nicely.

In another instant a bell rang and the gate doors flew open. A man's voice from the loudspeaker shouted, "And they're off!"

From the left came a thunder of hooves and blurred colored shirts. Twelve horses charged down the track for their first time past the finish line. People crowded at the fence and shouted out numbers. Molly craned her neck to find Dancer. She looked for Manny's blue and white silks as the first four horses shot past the finish line. She only saw red, green, yellow, and brown. More horses galloped past, and now she saw blue and white in the center of the pack. Dancer was holding his own somewhere around seventh place. The horses rounded the second rail and headed around the far end of the track. There was a blur of colors. People were screaming and imploring their selections to win.

"Oh man," the black woman who Rosa had spoken with earlier shouted, "that horse is going to finish dead last and I bet my two dollars."

Across the track a dark horse moved to the outside and passed two horses. Suddenly there was an opening and the horse filled the gap. Molly focused her binoculars.

"It's Dancer! He's in fourth. Look at him go!"

The horses crowded the rail. Molly couldn't see, but as they rounded into the homestretch there were three horses in front. One of the jockeys wore blue and white.

"Run, Baby!" the black woman shouted.

Rosa and Karen were shouting too.

"Go, Dancer!" Karen shouted.

The horses seemed to be moving in slow motion. A wall of noise rose around Molly as she watched the horses thundering closer. She could see Dancer on the inside on the rail and it looked like he might be blocked.

Manny's hand was in the air and the crop came down, once, twice, three times. Dancer seemed to bolt to the left, move between the two other horses and, break out in front of them. Molly held her breath. Dancer's head was down, legs churning, and ears flat back. He was ahead by two lengths. He stretched. His tail flew in the wind. At the pole, Dancer led by four lengths. Manny raised his fist in the air. The black woman and Rosa were locked in a hug jumping up and down. Molly was crying. Karen was smiling widely and patting Molly's head. Men near them were tossing betting slips to the ground. "Who the heck is Dashaway Dancer?" a man asked. "Fifteen-to-one. I can't believe it."

Molly, Rosa and Karen rushed down to the paddock arriving just as Marty, Manny, and Dancer entered the winner's circle. Manny hoisted up a bouquet of flowers in the shape of a horseshoe. Cameras flashed for the photo op. Manny looked younger and was beaming with pride. Dancer seemed bored. He knew he would win and he lifted his massive head to pose for pictures. This was a great moment for 3-M Farm. Molly smiled as she looked at the program and realized for the first time that she was listed as one of Dancer's owners.

"Baby girl," Marty said to his daughter. "We just won two thousand dollars, and, minus expenses, we're fifteen hundred ahead. Thanks to you. Thanks to you. Oh, this is great. I never thought we could win. We're going out for gigantic steaks. Nice work, Manny. You really brought him in that last furlong."

"Are you kidding?" Manny said. "He was bringing me. Man, did he kick out at the end. He wanted it. Oh Dancer, you big beautiful boy."

In the next month Dancer ran four more times and took two firsts, a second by a nose, and a dead heat for third place. Once again, Dancer was the prime moneymaker for 3-M Farm. Marty Grimaldi paid off bills and loans. By the end of the summer Manny's home was paid off and he had shiny new silks for the fall season. Marty bought a two-place horse trailer in great condition and four horses and another ten cows were added to the livestock. Marty told everyone that Molly was responsible for Dancer's return by using psychology on him, and tricking him into becoming a winner again.

Manuel and Rosa were married in September. Their wedding was like a colorful, beautiful Mexican festival. They would be living at the farm now and this gave Molly opportunity to ask Marty about his intentions.

"Say Dad, I wonder if another married couple will be living at the farm in the near future."

"Why Molly, are you and Danny getting married?"

"Come on, Dad. I think you should make your move soon. Karen's the woman in the black dress. She's the one all the farmers and country boys are getting ready to line up for, if she remains unspoken for."

"She is a looker, isn't she?"

"Yeah, she's a looker, sure enough. She's about the best looking woman in Ocala."

"What makes you think she would marry me?"

"I don't know. I'll go ask her."

"No!"

"You're right. You go ask her."

"Not now, Molly."

"So you admit you've been thinking about it?"

"No, I haven't been thinking about it. Manny and Rosa have been going together for six years."

"You're going to wait six years?"

"I might not ask her at all. Molly, are you saying you want me to get married?"

"I'm in no hurry, but you better had be. Someone like Karen won't last long."

"Okay, I'll go ask her."

"Really?"

"No, but I sure will consider all possibilities. You may not have thought of this, but helping us with Dancer is now going to pay off for you."

"How so?"

"Dancer has made it possible for us to make our bills and invest in the future. Manny wouldn't have married Rosa if he couldn't give her a good life."

"What does that have to do with me?"

"It has everything to do with you. Rosa is a very hard worker and she'll do most of the cooking and the laundry."

"For all of us?"

"You cooked and cleaned for all of us. Now Rosa will do so many of the chores you had to do. I never liked you doing so much and now you'll be able to concentrate on homework, Augie, and being a kid instead of always having to be an adult."

"What about Rosa?"

"She's excited to help and she'll do less than she did before coming here. She was cooking for thirty people on that farm where she lived and you should have seen the cabin she shared with three other women. This is good for everyone and you helped make it happen. Whatever led you to your idea about Dancer?"

"Horses and people aren't that much different. They want food and safety and comfort, but just like us, they have to have a reason for being alive. They want to be important and that's what Dancer lost. He wasn't important anymore. Dad, realistically we are good for now, but Dancer can't race forever."

"I know that, but the more he wins the more we get for breeding fees. One of those colts I bought is quite a runner. Manny has been taking a long look at the chestnut. We got him cheaply and then there's Augie. Your little colt has lots of possibilities."

"I don't know if I want Augie to race."

"You've been training him. He's already close to six hundred pounds of all muscle."

"I keep thinking about what Doc said."

"I thought you put that away months ago."

"I never forget anything Doc said."

"I see, but let's not go there tonight. Tonight we celebrate Manny's marriage and our good fortune. Over there, you see that niece of Rosa's talking to Danny? She's got her eye on him. I think she thinks he's kind of a looker too."

"You think Danny will like her if she has a black eye?"

"I see. So, which of us will get married first?"

"The way you're going, who knows? I'm going over to have dessert with Danny."

Molly and Danny took their plates filled with several Mexican dessert specialities out to a picnic table in front of the small rented hall.

"Are you having a good time?" Molly asked.

"Are you kidding? The food is wonderful and the people are happy and carefree. The weddings I've been to were all the same. The bride and groom walk around and shake hands and act stiff and proper. Did you see what was happening when we left? Rosa was carrying Manny up on the stage. Also, it is great that I get to be with you."

"Well, thank you."

"I never saw you wear a dress before and you're wearing lipstick and stuff."

"I hate it."

"You shouldn't. You are beautiful."

CHAPTER SIXTEEN

A City Boy and A Country Girl

Molly turned fourteen at the end of November and her life was never better. Dancer won a major race at missing the track record by only seven seconds and Manny was being touted as "Jockey of the Year." The only thing that would hurt his chances was that he rode only the Dancer. Other jockeys rode a variety of mounts. Molly couldn't make the trip to see that race because of school. It was wonderful news and she and Rosa danced in the kitchen. Her father apologized for missing his daughter's birthday for the very first time.

"I'll make it up to you," he said. "We have a race at Churchill Downs on the way home and we have a good chance to be invited to the Derby if we win."

"The Kentucky Derby?"

"You bet," her father said. "Dancer is actually too old for the Derby, but he has an outside chance. The important thing is he has taken us out of the red and into the black. With both orange groves doing well and Dancer's success, 3-M is in great shape. You and Rosa doing okay?"

"We're great. Karen took us out to dinner for my birthday and Danny came with us."

"You and Danny getting married for your birthday?"

"We might for one of them, but not this one. He gave me a LeAnn Rimes CD and a rose."

"Did he give you a little kiss?'"

"Oh no, Dad," Molly answered. "He gave me a great big 'kissee'—lasted about an hour and a half."

"He'll be swinging around on the weathervane," Marty said into the phone. "Did he really?"

"He kissed me—yeah," Molly said quietly. "It lasted about two seconds—is that okay?"

"Yes, it's okay."

"Good. In that case, it lasted two minutes."

"I don't worry about Danny."

"He worries about you."

"He does?"

"Oh yeah," Molly said. "He thinks you're a cross between John Wayne and Marshall Dillon."

"Let's not let him think anything else. Before Manny gets on the phone with Rosa, tell Karen I'll call her tonight. Oh, one more thing—go out in the barn and look in the burlap bag in the back of the tack room. It's behind a four by eight piece of plywood. There's a little present for you. You didn't think I'd forget, did you? You will always be my baby and my best friend. We've been through it all together, haven't we?"

"Yes, we have."

"Go get your present. It's a nice matching dress with high heel shoes. The bonus is the little purse with rhinestones. It's fab. You'll love the look."

"Oh, stop it."

"Well, you're fourteen now. I guess we need to put the jeans and boots aside and give some nice dresses and cut your hair and take you to some modeling classes."

"So, what did you get me?"

"Just go look. You don't have to call me back. Manny and I will be on the road after he tells Rosa he loves her a couple hundred times. Happy birthday, Molly. You're the finest person I have ever known."

"I love you, Dad. Good luck at Churchill. Okay, here's Rosa."

Molly went straight out to the barn. With all the hustle and bustle of Manny's wedding and Dancer's races, Molly figured her father had forgotten her birthday and she wasn't about to mention it. Marty had tried so hard to be both mother and father he had to be forgiven little things, and Molly had decided if he had forgotten her birthday it would be considered a little thing. He had gone to some trouble to hide her gift and Molly wrestled with a big piece of plywood and saw a giant burlap bag with a bow on it. Molly fell to her knees and untied the twist tie holding the bag.

"Oh wow!" she shouted as she pulled a brand new western saddle from a lowly burlap bag. It was one hundred per cent leather and the stirrups had stout wooden cuffs. The horn was brass and shined to a high gloss. This was first quality. It was only now she noticed the back pads had been lettered probably by a craftsman. It was a perfect job. On one side, burned right into the leather, it said "Molly Grimaldi" and on the other side, with quotation marks around them, were the words "Handsome Augie." Not only had her father remembered her birthday, this gift had taken weeks of planning and the best part was he had probably purchased the saddle before Dancer won his first race. She took the saddle back to Augie's stall and tossed it over the railing to get a better look. She had seen saddles as nice as this one at horse shows, but never a farm or ranch. The best saddle she had seen until now was the one Grace used. The handiwork on it was nothing compared to this.

Molly raced back to the house to see if Rosa was still on the phone. She wanted to thank her father but it was too late. Rosa was off the phone and had already cleaned the breakfast dishes and was ready to go back to the mobile home. Instead, Molly half dragged her out to see the new saddle.

"Oh, it is a very fancy one, no?"

"Oh, it's a very fancy one, yes," Molly said. Now Rosa and Augie looked at the names burned into the leather. "I know my dad must have spent a lot of money on it."

"Mr. Martin loves you very much. Manuel tells me about the saddle a couple months ago, but this is the first time I have seen it. It is so beautiful. I like the way the leather is different colors, you know? Here it is very deep brown and then it is lighter at the top, and look at this saddle horn. This is brass?"

"I think so," Molly said. "It'll last forever."

"Look at how Augie sniffs at it," Rosa said. "I think he likes it."

"Until we put it on his back. I've gotten him used to blankets especially here in this stall, but I doubt he'll like anything on his back while he's out in the corrals or in the meadow. He'll need to learn. Rosa, are you happy here?"

"I love it very much. Manuel and I are so happy. We have the nice new home and I get to cook for you and Mr. Martin."

"That's okay with you?"

"This is a very good life for me. I love to cook and the laundry is so much easier. On the other ranch, I cook and do laundry for thirty men. I have no dryer and hang the clothes out on the lines—thirty jeans, thirty shirts, and a thousand socks. It was very hard work. It's okay with you that Rosa is here? This is your home and now Rosa comes into your kitchen and uses your washer and dryer."

"Rosa, you can use our stove, washer, and dryer any time. I might feel differently if you were riding my horse and dating Danny, but I'm thrilled to have you here and I thank you for taking on some of my chores without complaining."

"I have no complaints."

"I sure don't. You have to teach me how to cook all the great things you make. I know my dad and Manny are tired of cornbread, potatoes, and meat, but those are the only things I know how to make."

Rosa left to complete her many chores at home and Molly again looked at her saddle, sure that it would be her last tomboy kind of gift from her father. Next year she would be fifteen. She wanted a computer of her own. Maybe she could sell the idea to her father and Manny by showing them all the ways a computer could help on the farm. Marty had resisted buying a computer as if it would somehow change 3-M with new technology. It was a ridiculous argument, considering the tractors and milking machines were state of the art. Manny's fertilizers and spraying and irrigation machines were updated regularly. Molly hoped that if the Dancer finished in the money on the way home, there would be a conversation about joining the present century. If she could find extra time at school to run programs specific to 3-M Farm, even Manny and her father might be convinced of its necessity. She could chart feeding schedules; create spread sheets on which crops turned the most profit, and she might even be able to predict which animals should be bought or sold. The saddle was a great choice for now, especially when a horse like Augie might live thirty years or more, but the Grimaldis needed a computer and she would wait for good moods to bring up the subject.

Just because Dancer was out winning races didn't mean the other animals wouldn't be hungry. With her father and Manny out testing the racing circuit, Molly had more chores than hours in the day. Rosa was a wonderful helper, but Molly had to be sure the cows were milked and all the chicken eggs collected, crated and marked. Then the horses had to be brought in from the pasture and fed and watered. Molly ran from one task to the next. By the time she drove the jeep to check the fence lines and orange groves, she was exhausted. She checked the timers on Manny's water lines, flipped the main switch, and now huge plumes of water danced in the air for hundreds of feet. The water was timed to shut off in an hour. Manny's cherished vegetables would be moist and fresh. It was nearly dusk when Molly finished her chores and stopped in the barn to check on Grace and Augie. She thought about how experts try to figure out what causes teenagers to get in trouble. She had read articles that took aim at video games, MTV, television programs, or even computers. No one asked her. She would have said, "A cause for most teenager's problems is boredom. They look for something to do." Molly was too tired to be bored. She dragged herself into the house to call Danny before finishing her homework.

"Where have you been all weekend?" Danny asked.

"Dad and Manny are up country racing Dancer and I have to do all the chores."

"I would have come to help you."

"I hate to have you come to my house to make you work."

"It's fun just to be with you. I don't mind the work when we do it together. Don't you ever get mad?"

"At what?"

"That you have so much to do and other kids do almost nothing. I mean, I do almost nothing."

"I don't know, Danny. I don't have anything to compare my life against. A farm is different than a house. A farm is a living breathing thing and when helpless lives depend on you, there is a responsibility, you know?"

"Maybe it's the way I'm asking the question," Danny continued. "I'm asking if you get jealous of the kids in the subdivisions. Do you ever want to trade places?"

"I might if I knew what that life was all about. I just know what this life is about. Remember how I told you I was jealous of not getting to go places because of the farm? Yeah, I'd like to go to Disney World. It's probably only fifty miles away and I've never been there. I'd like to go to New York and Washington and maybe even Vegas when I get older. I think that's the hardest thing. There are no days off on a farm. Even when my mom was dying, my dad came home from the hospital and did chores carrying a lantern. A farm has to have constant care. Honest, sometimes I feel like I can feel the land breathing. I don't think I'd feel that way if I lived in a suburb. Is there a reason you're asking all this?"

"Well," Danny said, sounding secretive "there is a reason, but I can't tell you about it yet."

"Tell me about what?"

"I'm not going to tell you about it yet. I'll just say it's a good thing."

"Can you give me a hint?"

"Your dad wants you to take a day off."

"I don't understand."

"Good. Your dad and I had a little talk and he said I could have you."

"He said you could have me?"

"For a day."

"Are you going to tell me any more?"

"No, I can't. I just want to say that I used to think I was good with girls, but I'm not good with you. Even in Baltimore I had girlfriends right away. I think it was because I was the new kid, but with you it's kind of like a dog chasing a car."

"Excuse me?"

"The dog never figures out what he'll do if he catches the car. I don't know what to do about you."

"Is that a good thing?"

"It's a great thing—at least it is for me. It's like you're fourteen, but you're really thirty. When you talk about the land and stuff, I feel like a little kid. My life isn't wrong, but yours is so right. I like the way you look at things and people. Don't you notice that I'm so careful with you?"

"You mean like that you never try stuff?"

"Well, yes, that's part of it. I want to kiss you and be with you. You have no idea how beautiful you are and that makes you more beautiful. That makes me really careful to respect you. I think I'm doing a crummy job of explaining this."

"You're doing fine."

"Molly, I'm just saying I'm happy just to be around you, and, since you're a girl and my friend..."

"Are you asking if I consider you my boyfriend?"

"Yes."

"Yes, I do, if that's okay."

"Are you kidding? You mean if someone asked you if you had a boyfriend, you would say 'Danny'?"

"Yes, I would say 'Danny'."

"That is so cool. I'm Molly Grimaldi's boyfriend."

"You are so cute."

"I am?"

"You know you are, Danny Freeman. That's why you had all those girlfriends in Baltimore. You figure this open announcement will hurt our relationship?"

"See, that's what I meant months ago when I worried that I met you too early. By the way, I didn't have all those girlfriends. I just meant it was always easy for me to have a girlfriend because I was new in town and I knew I wouldn't be staying a long time. My dad moves all around the country. This time, though, I think we're staying. Now I really hope so. Man! I'm Molly Grimaldi's boyfriend."

"Oh stop it. If it's such a big deal, how come you're one of the first to apply for the job?"

"I'm sure lots of people would love to be your boyfriend and I hope I'm enough to hang onto someone like you."

"Danny."

"I mean it. The jeans and ponytails don't hide you. You are beautiful, but too complicated for the average fourteen year old to have sense enough to want."

"I'm complicated?"

"Only in the way that most girls convince themselves they need a boyfriend. Molly has to want one to make the time available. There's a difference."

"Danny, I didn't even want a boyfriend until I met you. I can be a real disappointment. I can't do all the things the other girls can. I've been to one dance and that was only because you were there. I can't go to shows or hang out at the malls. It'll be hard for us to spend time together."

"Molly, I spend time with you even when you aren't around. You do and say things that just knock me out and then I can't think of anything else."

"For example?"

"For example, no girl has ever told me she feels connected to the land. City girls don't talk that way because they don't think that way. You say things like other people think the same thing, but they don't."

"And that means?"

"And that means I want to be connected to you. I don't know how to explain. It's like the day we went fishing you

173

knew how to sneak up on the fish. You wouldn't even let me put my shadow on the water because it might spook the fish. No girl would have thought of that."

"Do you like me enough to tell me the secret you have with my dad?"

"Nope, I won't be telling you that. I need your dad to like me. I need him to trust me, too. I'm not fooling with a real-life cowboy."

"You consider my dad a cowboy?" Molly laughed. "He would say he's a farmer."

"Oh no. Your dad is a cowboy. He walks like a cowboy. He talks like a cowboy. You could put him in a western movie and he would fit right in. He doesn't say much, but I'm not missing anything he says."

"Are you afraid of my dad?"

"Not yet, but I could be. Right now, he's more a hero. Don't tell my dad."

"He's a hero to me, too. He's really a gentle guy until something riles him."

"I won't rile him," Danny said. "No, I don't want to rile the cowboy."

"Danny, I have to run to do homework or some teachers will be riled."

"I know. I don't call all the times I'd like to. You know what?"

"What?"

"I'm Molly Grimaldi's boyfriend."

"That's a good thing?"

"That's a great thing."

CHAPTER SEVENTEEN

A New Computer on the Farm

Dancer didn't win at Churchill Downs. He was crowded onto the rail and in the backstretch another rider used his crop on Manny. There was no investigation even though there were crop marks across Manny's face. The good news was that the Dancer never quit. Even when Manny was nearly thrown off his back, Dancer kept digging and stretching and he moved from seventh to fourth at the finish line. Manny was furious and Marty Grimaldi laughed as he told the story of Manny later chasing the other rider all around the paddock until the jockey jumped in a waiting car and sped away.

"It was like they were still racing," Marty said. "Manny handed me Dancer's reins and then he takes off after the guy."

"Oh, Boss," Manny said, "if I got my hands on him and I would have ridden him a few furlongs. I hate a cheater."

"But the other horse didn't win, did he?" Molly asked.

"It was some kind of setup," Marty said. "Adults cheat. I think there was a payoff. They thought the Dancer would walk away, and someone paid someone to block his path."

"They do that?" Molly asked.

"Only the worst do that. We will be patient."

"Are you going to look for the guy?"

"I will," Manny said, "but you have to understand he did what someone had him do. It hurt your father and me more than Dancer. He knew something was happening, but he never stopped running. Bless his heart. He's a good one. There will be another day."

This was not the time to bring up the computer. The outside world was a great deal different than life on 3-M farm. Molly was furious and concerned about why her father and Manny took the whole thing so lightly.

"Don't you think you should have had an investigation?" She demanded.

"I saw the film. The horses were very close. It wasn't conclusive that the guy was going for Manny's face. I believe Manny. If Dancer hadn't been crowded out that jockey wouldn't have been close enough to do what he did. He was riding an average mount. That means as a jockey he was run-of-the-mill, a nobody. We save ourselves for bigger battles, Molly."

"I'm trying to understand, but I sure don't."

"You're fourteen. I can't get you to understand everything yet. I want you to be outraged when people don't play fairly, but you have to channel anger into a plan. Right now, the people at Churchill don't think Dancer is fast. He runs a forty thousand dollar claiming race there next month. I have a feeling there will be a nice surprise."

"Nope, I refuse to understand this. I know you might surprise them next month, but that doesn't explain what happened here. I refuse to accept this."

Marty stopped trying to tell Molly of the plan or explain the breaks of life to her. Her mind was made up. If she would have seen the man whip Manny, she would have chased him herself. No one hurt the people she loved. She stomped out of the barn to feed Augie. As she cooled down, she remembered the saddle and ran back to hug and thank her father.

"Are you the same person who was going to beat up a jockey a few minutes ago?" Marty asked as Molly locked him in a ferocious hug. "I gather you like the saddle."

"And the man who gave it to me," Molly said. "Dad, it's gorgeous."

"I had a hard time deciding what to get. I spent a long time considering a jockey saddle and settled on a show saddle. You catching my meaning here?"

"I think so. You don't think Augie should run, do you?"

"Let me be very clear on this, Molly. From the moment he drew breath, Augie has been, and will be, your horse. Your great granddaddy would have put him down. My father would have put him down. I couldn't put him down and maybe I was weak. So far, he is a wonderful horse and what happens to him from now on is for you to decide. I think you should show him and breed him and that way you'll have him for years. If he races, there are no guarantees. If you decide otherwise once you can ride him, I'll not argue. Like my dad used to say, he runs 'like a scalded dog.' I can't deny that. He's almost a thousand pounds and that leg holds up well. I won't deny that."

"But you bought a western saddle."

"I just wanted you to know, I'll understand if you run him. If he's as quick with a rider on top, it'll be hard to convince him he shouldn't run. He could be almost as fast as Dancer."

"I have time to decide. If he has power, I won't take it from him. I'll tell you that right now. I know what you are saying and I remember what Doc said, but if he's bound to run I won't stop him."

"You saying that for him or for you?"

"I don't understand."

"It'll come to you," her father said in his way of ending a conversation. "For now, we saddle break him and then you'll have a while to decide. He's almost two now and you can start letting him run with a saddle a few weeks before we think about riding him. When the time comes, Manny will help you. You won't find anyone better."

"Can I change the subject a little?" Molly asked. "This is likely a bad time for me to ask especially when you just shelled out for the saddle."

"You want a car?"

"If you're offering, I'll take a Mustang convertible—red or black."

"I'm not buying a you a car. When you get your license, you can have the jeep."

"Dad, the jeep has only one door. Out on the road, I don't know if it qualifies as a car."

"You were just talking about how Augie loves to run. You could ride him around."

"You figure they have hitching posts at college?"

"In the last two minutes we've gone from racing Augie to zooming down the turnpike in a Mustang. My life is flashing by just sitting on the porch."

"I want a computer."

"Well, say what you think, Molly," her father answered. "Did you say maybe you want a computer?"

"We need a computer, Dad."

"So, now we need a computer."

"We really do, Dad. I could teach you how to use it and you'll be amazed how many ways it will help on the farm."

"We're not getting a computer."

"That's unreasonable. I just want to talk about it and you say, 'We're not getting a computer.' Can't we talk it over? We usually talk about things. We could use a computer. Okay, I could use a computer. We could get a used one. All the other kids have a computer."

"You have never used that one until now," her father said, laughing out loud. "You have never used the 'All the other kid's' defense until this very minute. That's too funny. We're not getting a computer."

"Just tell me why not and I'll run along," Molly said. She stood defiantly in front of her father. She was facing him and not backing away. It was enough he should just say no without explanation, but now he was laughing. Grimaldis didn't do that.

"We aren't getting a computer because we don't need one."

"Who says we don't need one?"

"I do. Karen has a computer and you can use hers."

"Oh, that's great. I'll just jump on a horse and ride to Karen's every time I have computer work to do. Okay, Dad, I'm done with this conversation."

"You wouldn't have to do all that," her father said.

"Do all what?"

"Ride all the way to Karen's to use the computer. If you're following me here, that computer might be right here in the house. That's why there wouldn't be any need to go riding all the way over there. That's why we wouldn't need to buy a computer."

"You are making no sense," Molly said. "You sit there with that big smile and you talk about how we have a computer but we don't have a computer. Then we have Karen's computer and now Karen doesn't have a computer."

"Keep talking, Molly. Karen's not giving up her computer. It'll come to you."

"Dad," Molly said, sitting back on the porch stairs holding her face in her freckled hands, "how can we have a computer and Karen still has her computer? I don't get it. She wouldn't give us her computer and then come over to use it. Oh, wait a minute. Wait a minute! The only way we have a computer and Karen has the same one is...Dad, you're going to marry her?"

"Only if you approve and she'll have me."

"She doesn't know yet?"

"I haven't asked her yet. First this is Grimaldi business. You know nothing happens without you."

"You haven't asked her?"

"I have to ask you first."

"Well, get to it, Dad! I approve! You're going to get married. I'm so happy. Who could be better?"

"No one," her father said.

"You bet—no one! This is great. You're serious, right?"

"As serious as a hurricane. I thought it over long and hard. I kept asking myself, 'How am I going to get my little girl a computer?' Then it came to me."

"Oh hush," Molly said, jumping in her father's lap. "How are you going to do it?"

"What?"

"Ask her to marry you. Are you going to get down on your arthritic knees and say, 'Oh, my darling...'"

"Stop it."

"Oh my darling," Molly continued. "Please marry me and come to our ranch and fix all our critters. Please bring your computer. Please say 'Yes' and give me a little 'kissee'."

"And you say I tease you. What do you really think? You think she'll want to marry me?"

"I'm a little prejudiced, but I think she would have married you months ago. A woman can see how another woman looks at a man."

"Oh, yeah?"

"Oh, yeah. She's got the big eyes for you. She'll start unplugging the computer before you finish the question. By the way, how do you know she would move here?"

"We kind of talked about it once. I said it would be great to build a new building and have animals come here for boarding and veterinarian work. We could take on dogs and cats. You even talked about that."

"Did you buy a ring?"

"Yep, Manny and I went to the jewelers in New York."

"Do I get to see it?"

"Do you mind if Karen sees it first?"

"No, you're right. She should have people to show it to. Dad, I'm very happy about this. I am."

"Do you feel it is somehow unfair to your mom?"

"Wow, there's a question. I think I feel we have room in our hearts for everyone who deserves a special place. I think mom's place in our hearts will always be there, but lives are like chapters in a book. I'm good with this and I think mom understands."

"You say that in present tense."

"Yes, I do," Molly said firmly.

"Molly, some of these new chapters scare me."

"Don't let Danny hear you're afraid of anything. Now I won't have to be an old woman staying on the farm with her lonely old dad."

"So, now that I might be getting married, you would move off the farm?"

"You'll have to kick me off this farm. As a matter of fact, someday I hope to have a house built over by the pond with my own driveway to the road. What would you and Karen think of that?"

"All of my life is tied to your happiness," Marty said, "You'd consider doing that?"

"I plan on doing that."

"You know," Marty said, "I guess it would have never come to all this unless Karen came home after her father died. I just wish Doc could be here for the wedding."

"He'll be there," Molly said, jumping to her feet. "I have to go tell Augie the news."

CHAPTER EIGHTEEN

Disney World and Mars

Every day going into Christmas vacation, Molly made sure that Augie got to feel the saddle on his back. At first, he hated it. The first time she made the mistake of taking the saddle out to the corral thinking he would accept it as he had accepted blankets in his stall, but the moment he felt the weight he went berserk. He reared and threw the saddle off his back. He whirled around and stomped at it. He was nearly full-grown and he was angry. He snorted and ran the circle of the corral. He came back and tried to grab the saddle horn in his mouth. He dashed around for another attack. Molly ran in, grabbed the saddle, and threw it over the fence. Now she put the saddle on Augie's back only when he was in his stall. He still didn't like it, but if an apple or sugar cube followed it, he tolerated the saddle a little longer each day. It took nearly a month before he would allow the cinches to be loosely tied. Breaking Augie wasn't easy.

Soon Karen became an important part of 3-M Farm. She flashed a diamond ring and she and Molly shared long talks about how lives would be changed for the better. To Molly, she would remain 'Karen' and if Molly ever called her 'Mom' it would have to be Molly's choice. For the most part, Molly was happy to leave wedding plans to the adults while she focused on school, Augie, and Danny. It was a calm and comfortable time. Dancer did his part and won the big claiming race by four lengths.

The Saturday before Christmas, Molly smelled breakfast cooking and heard the hiss of sausage frying in the big skillet. She thought Rosa must have been up early. She heard Manny and her father laughing and talking in the kitchen. Molly showered, pulled on fresh jeans and her work boots.

She usually started the day in a flannel shirt to allow for crisp mornings, then, if the December sun worked the temperatures up into the seventies, she changed to short sleeves. She used the blow dryer until her hair was nearly dry, then switched to a brush to make sure her hair wasn't snarled. Usually her hair would be completely dry after just a few minutes in the sun. Today, she emerged from the bedroom to Marty, Manny, and Rosa laughing at her.

"You aren't wearing that, are you?" her father asked.

"It's what I wear. What's wrong with it?"

"You aren't wearing such an outfit today?" Manny asked, joining in the fun.

"What's the matter with you people?" Molly asked. "What should I be wearing?"

"Oh, I think a dress," Rosa suggested.

"No, not a dress," her father said, talking more to Rosa than to Molly. "I think the jeans are okay to start, but maybe she should have shorts in a duffle bag. Definitely no boots—tennis shoes on a day like this, don't you think, Manny?"

"Oh yes. Tennis shoes would be the thing to wear."

"What's going on?"

"Go put on tennis shoes and a lighter shirt and then we'll tell you."

"Tell me now."

"Nope," Marty said. "First go change and then we'll talk."

Molly did as she was told, then reappeared, turned around slowly and stretched out her arms as if asking if she was now more appropriate.

"Oh, that's much better," Marty said. Manny and Rosa nodded. "Now sit down and grab some breakfast. You don't have much time."

"Time for what?"

"Hurry, hurry, Molly. Eat some toast. They'll be here soon."

"Who's going to be here?"

"Danny and his family. You have the day off, young lady. You're going on a road trip. Oops, here they are now. There's money under your plate. You're going to need it."

"Why are they here?" Molly asked but now the dining room was already empty. Molly thought clearly this had to do with the secret Danny never mentioned a second time. The Freemans were standing in front of a beautiful white Lincoln. Mother and father had on ridiculously loose Bermuda shorts and looked like tourists, but Danny and his sister Andrea both wore jeans, t-shirts and big smiles. Molly stepped out on the porch and stared at all of them.

"Doesn't she know what's going on?" Danny asked.

"No, I don't," Molly said, knowing she was flushed and that her freckles must be really bright, "What is going on?"

"Molly," Danny said, "you're going to Disney World!"

"You're kidding?"

"Jump in!" Mr. Freeman shouted. "We're on our way."

"You get your money?" Marty whispered.

"Dad, thank you. What about my chores?"

"Karen's coming over. You're unemployed today."

"This is great."

Molly sat in the back of the finest car she had ever seen and she noticed she could barely feel a bounce from the dip in the driveway as they drove under the 3-M sign.

Soon they were out on the highway and headed for Orlando. The Freemans were easy to talk to and Mrs. Freeman seemed especially glamorous. Each time she rested her arm on the seat behind her husband, Molly couldn't help but notice the diamond ring twice the size of the one her father had gotten for Karen. Even more impressive, her fingers were long and delicate and each fingernail was perfectly painted with rose-colored polish. Molly instinctively looked at her own hands and they were rough looking by comparison. Her nails were clipped to the quick and seemed to have ridges and lines where Mrs. Freeman's were smooth and feminine. Molly folded her hands in her lap and smiled as Danny pointed at the Disney World signs spaced along the highway.

"Danny tells me you have a fast little horse," Mrs. Freeman said.

"Yes, ma'am," Molly answered, "his name is Augie. He's just a colt now, but he's very fast."

"Are you the one who races him?"

"I will be, but he's not old enough to be ridden yet. My father has a racehorse named Dancer. He's the one that races. He's Augie's father."

"So, Augie will race when he gets older?"

"I hope he will," Molly said, deciding not to tell the long story about Augie's leg. "I hope to ride him."

"You will be the jockey?"

"I hope so. I need to watch my weight."

"You're in perfect shape."

"To be a jockey, you really need to stay under a hundred twenty pounds. I'm pretty close right now."

"Do you have a jockey outfit and everything?"

"As a matter of fact, I do. I had some silks given to me by an old friend."

"Silks?" Danny asked.

"Yeah, the shiny satin shirts jockeys wear are called 'silks'."

"Wouldn't you be afraid to run with all those horses?" Andrea asked. "It looks dangerous."

"I don't know. I've never done it. I've raced one horse against another on our little track, but Manny will teach me. If I can't ride Augie, Manny will."

"Who is Manny?" Mr. Freeman asked as he drove amid more cars than Molly had ever seen.

"Manny is the little man you met at the farm. Don't let his size fool you. He's a jockey giant and one of the best riders in the country."

Soon the Freemans' Lincoln passed International Drive and then followed the signs pointing to Disney World. There were towering hotels left and right and a place called "Wet and Wild" that featured water slides higher than the buildings around them. There were signs everywhere.

Mr. Freeman parked in the 'Mickey' lot and Molly and the Freemans rode a tram and the Magic Kingdom just ahead. There were thousands of people converging on the ticket windows. The scene reminded Molly of racetracks, except here were so many children. She was pleased to have her own money. Had the Freemans paid her way she should have been embarrassed the entire day. Molly wondered how her father could have known it would cost so much. She would remind him it should count as the majority of her Christmas gifts. Molly handed twenty dollar bills to the clerk, and was amazed that people paid so much to have a good time for a single day.

It was a wonderful gift and a perfect day. Molly loved the parades and the castles and all the rides. The 'Haunted House' was her favorite and 'It's a Small World' played a song that she hummed most of the day. Things were done on such a grand scale and continued with hoisting big goblets at lunch in the

Magic Castle Restaurant. There, Danny surprised her with a Minnie Mouse shirt and she slipped into the bathroom and put it on so Danny could see her wearing it. At dark there was another parade and this one featured twinkling lights and all the Disney characters. Danny held her hand as she stood on tiptoes trying to miss nothing. She slept on Danny's shoulder most of the way home and each time her eyes opened even for a second he was looking at her and smiling. It was a perfect day and night and nearly one in the morning before she arrived home. Manny and Rosa's trailer was dark, but there was a light on in the big house where she knew her father would be waiting to be sure she arrived home safely. Rarely did they spend time apart, especially with Molly being the one away from home. As the car negotiated the ruts in the driveway, Marty came out in jeans and a t-shirt. His hair was rumpled. He looked tired.

"So, did everyone have a great time?" he asked as he grabbed the duffel bag Mr. Freeman retrieved from the trunk. "Did you get enough Mickey to last a while?"

"I got enough Mickey to last a lifetime," Mr. Freeman said.

After appropriate thank-yous, the Freeman car eased down the dirt road to the blacktop. Molly and her father sat on the porch and soon the smell of cherry pipe tobacco filled the misty air. Molly prattled on and on about the wonders of Disney World and Marty patted his daughter's head as she included every detail of her big day. She thanked him again and again. Abruptly the Grimaldis fell quiet. Father and daughter looked at a curtain of stars and a face on the moon. It was as quiet as Disney was loud. Now Molly whispered.

"I'm sorry you and Karen had to do all my chores."

"I'm sorry you have so many chores to do. Augie's fine, but I think he missed you. He stayed in the corral most of the day and every time the door opened he came to the fence to see if it was you. Karen went out and threw apples for him, but he seemed a little slower than usual. It's not fun for him unless you throw them. Otherwise, it was a quiet day."

"Yeah?"

"I have to admit each time Karen or Rosa came out the door, I looked to see if it might be you."

"Thank you."

"I'm not going to lose you to the big city?"

"Nice place to visit, but I don't want to live there."

"Thank you. You are pretty special, Molly Grimaldi. You sleep in, baby girl. You must be really tired."

"It's a nice kind of tired," Molly said, looking up at the stars. "What's that bright star by the moon? I don't remember that one."

"Believe it or not—that's Mars. Only once every sixty thousand years does it come this close to earth."

"We'll probably miss it next time, huh?"

"I'm afraid—everything has a time and a season. At least we were born at the right time to see it now. They didn't have Mars at Disney World, did they?"

"Nope, they sure didn't. Ladies and gentlemen, presenting from the Grimaldi porch: the planet Mars."

"You go on to bed, Ms. Molly. I'm going to have a few more minutes with Mars."

"Disney's twinkling lights have nothing on ours," Molly said.

"I hope you always feel that way."

"No doubt in my mind," Molly said. She kissed her father, and went off to bed. She was sound asleep in seconds.

CHAPTER NINETEEN

Young Champions

All through Christmas vacation, Augie wore his saddle every day. He didn't like it; he tolerated it. He was a gorgeous horse, and Molly snapped pictures that she would tape in his stall with the others she had taken from the week he was born until this very day. She wondered if Augie could understand the pictures as himself and see the difference between when he was a helpless one hundred pound foal to the magnificent colt he was now. Augie was as black as coal ash and his white star was more prominent than his father's and as white as a wedding gown with the same satin look. Nearing his second birthday, he was now over one thousand pounds and his back legs were pitched high and rippled with muscle. He was raised at the withers. Like a true stallion, his neck was long and sloped and veins bulged at the surface on the side of his face. His eyes were brown and bright, his nostrils large and flared, his mane long and silky, and the taper of his great chest gave way to long and straight muscled front legs. He was a perfect stallion specimen and looked every bit a thoroughbred. With his show saddle adorned with his name on one side and Molly's the other, he would be the perfect horse for a television star to ride into the sunset.

Whenever Manny brought Dancer out for a workout, Molly would saddle Augie and make him watch from the sidelines. Augie would train his eyes on his father and each time Dancer passed on the dead run, Augie nodded his approval. When Dancer walked off his run, Molly would release Augie onto the track and father and son would walk along together. A year ago, Augie looked tiny next to Dancer, but now the two were nearly the same size. Augie would nuzzle and challenge Dancer and every now and then Dancer would snort and bop

Augie under the chin hard enough to hear Augie's teeth click. Dancer was boss and he would take only so much—even from his own son.

Amazing Grace was different. Molly would ride the palomino and Augie would prance alongside pestering and challenging. Every now and then Molly would break off into a sprint and, in a flash, Augie would be right next to her. He was clearly much faster than his mother now, and he enjoyed toying with her and pressing his advantage of strength and speed. Grace tolerated him with calmness and disinterest. He would never try the same things with the Dancer. One morning after waiting for Augie to be exhausted from running and teasing, Marty called Molly to bring her colt to the chute.

"You walk him in and I'll crosstie him," Marty said.

"What are we going to do?"

"Augie's not going to like his too much. I'll hold him and you sit. Easy. Okay, let your weight come down."

Immediately, Augie tried to whirl his head around but the crossties held him. Now he kicked out with his back legs and Molly held on for dear life. Augie was making braying sounds Molly had never heard from him before. After a few minutes of coaxing and calming, he stood still with Molly on his back. Molly leaned down and whispered and Augie was still, but his ears were laid back. If he had the chance he would bolt in a heartbeat. Molly knew it.

"Alright, come off him now—nice an gentle. We'll do it again tomorrow."

True to his word, Marty Grimaldi arrived just after Augie seemed tuckered out chasing Grace all around the corral. This time Marty carried a helmet and he motioned for Molly to bring Augie around to the chute. This time Marty cinched the saddle tight. He hooked either side of Augie's bridle to the crossties and he checked the bit to make sure it was secure.

"You want me to do this?"

"No, sir."

"He's going to try to throw you. You know that, don't you?"

"I know that. Any suggestions?"

"Well, if you know you're going off, be sure to clear the stirrups. I don't want him to drag you. Man, I'd rather let you loose in a car than this."

"He's tired, Dad. Maybe he'll go easy."

"I wouldn't count on it. You get this helmet on and stay as low to the saddle as you can. Molly, would you rather wait?"

"For him to get older and stronger? I don't think so. Today's the day."

"I'll hold him and you settle on his back a while. Then I'll walk him to the end of the chute and then it's up to you. I've seen some horses that just kept walking and everything is fine."

"You think Augie might be one of those?"

"No, I don't. You hold on like there's a canyon beneath you. You hear?"

Molly said nothing and tightened the helmet strap under her chin. Manny and Rosa stayed back up on the porch getting ready to come forward once Molly and Augie entered the corral. Molly sat gently on Augie's back and finally took her hands off the sidewalls so he could feel her full weight. Molly whispered to Augie as her father moved the ties up closer to the entrance of the corral. Moments later he moved Augie another six or eight feet. Ahead was the clear space of the corral.

"Last chance to bail out," he said, unbuckling first one crosstie and then the other. "We go?"

"Let it rip," Molly said with her teeth clenched.

Augie shot out of the corral as if from a gun and Molly was thrown backward by the sudden surge. In seconds, Augie reared, bolted, and suddenly all four legs seemed to be off the ground at the same time. He was running out of control and stopped only to rise up high in the air and then dash again to the other side of the corral. Molly looked like a rag doll and she saw her father and Manny in a blur. Abruptly she was snatched in another direction. Her right foot was caught in a stirrup and Augie tried to buck her off once-twice-three times. Slather formed on Augie's lips. Now he raced for the other end of the corral. Molly lost her grip on the reins. Marty and Manny were poised at the entrance should she fall and Augie try to stomp her. In a huge effort, Augie's legs seemed to splay out in all directions and Molly's face seemed to almost touch the ground. Her sweat soaked hair stuck to the side of her face. Still she hung on. It was a wild ride, Augie's hooves dug into the wet turf; dirt clods flew everywhere. Molly pleaded with Augie to slow down. She called his name again and again. Yet on Augie ran. He tried to turn quickly enough to fling her into the side rails. Suddenly, he slowed. Then, he just stopped. Augie and Molly were in the middle of the coral breathing heavily. Was Augie resting for another run? Whatever he would do, Molly was thankful for the rest. Marty, Manny, and Rosa remained quiet staring out to the center of the ring. Now Molly took the reins in her hands and shouted, "Augie, walk!"

"She did it!" Manny yelled. "She broke him."

Now Molly and her colt walked as one and Molly pulled him right and then left. She pulled back and Augie stopped. She kicked gently at his flanks and Augie walked. It was good.

"Can I breath now?" Marty asked. "Molly, what a great ride."

"I can't believe how strong he is," Molly said, still panting. "Now I see why they measure a car's strength by how much horsepower it has. Wow, he is so strong. I thought he was never going to stop."

"Me either," Marty said. "Now he is truly your horse."

"Will he remember tomorrow?"

"He'll test you again, but now he'll accept a rider. Let me change that. He'll accept you. I'm not even going to try to ride him. I can't believe you held on when he went low on you. Good ride, Molly."

For the next twenty minutes Molly walked her horse around the corral and the whole time she told him how wonderful he was. She jumped off and walked him to the water trough. Augie slurped as he drank. A tired Molly walked her colt back to the barn where finally the saddle and dreaded bit were both off and she brushed and curried him until he gentled enough for her to use a soft currycomb on his face and mane. She let him calm and gave him an apple. Augie seemed a pony again and he chomped the apple until sweet juices ran out the corners of his mouth.

"You're a tough guy, Mr. Augie. Did we have a big time today? Now we can ride everywhere we want. That'll be good, huh? You won't have to watch anymore. Can I tell you something? You scared the bejabbers out of me. I never knew you were so strong."

By June, Augie and Molly had ridden many times. It was second nature for him to accept Molly and a saddle. He liked to run free and easy out in the pasture and Molly would try to find smooth straight-aways where he could gallop a few hundred yards. He loved to run fast. It was difficult to get him to slow down. Sometimes he fought the bit just to run a while longer. Even when he was left alone in the east pasture he loved to scatter other horses and he would do all he could to get them to run. Then he would pass them as if they were rooted in place. He was faster that fast. Every rancher and farmer who saw him made ridiculous offers to buy him. Molly would listen to offers of thousands of dollars before announcing Augie was not for sale for any price.

Augie became so fond of riding that Molly had to remove his saddle and put it in the tack room. Every time Molly came into the barn Augie would bite at his saddle telling her he wanted to ride. It got to the point Molly worried he would break his teeth on the brass knob, so she finally just mounted the saddle on one of the props in the tack room so Augie wouldn't see it. With Rosa handling dinner, Molly could ride as soon as she got home from school. She was teaching Danny to ride on weekends and he had graduated to riding Amazing Grace. Manny was sure Grace was pregnant again, but she could be ridden several months into a pregnancy that would last eleven months. Right now, it was good for her to exercise and Saturday mornings were spent riding and fishing. Danny and Karen were the only outsiders allowed to pet Augie. He didn't like Rosa and wouldn't take an apple from Danny's father. He was acting more and more like a stallion. He was handsome and he knew it. He was fast and he knew it. He was Molly's horse and he knew that too.

During every run, Molly would excuse herself and let Augie cut loose for a couple hundred yards. Danny would watch in amazement as the blur that was reddish blonde hair and flying black mane dashed past him. Molly loved the sensation of traveling on horseback at speeds approaching thirty-five miles per hour and it wasn't a matter of showing off. Just like Augie, she loved to run and was becoming a better rider every day.

"Let me ask you a question," Danny said one day as they stopped for a half hour of fishing. "Today when you ran past me and Grace, you kind of dipped to the left. What happened there?"

"What did you say?"

"It seemed for a couple strides you got lower. What was that? Did you do that on purpose?"

"Danny," Molly said, "this is important. What exactly did you see?"

"Probably nothing, but it was like you froze for a stride or something. It just seemed like you dipped down a little or something."

"On the left side?"

"Yeah, it was like you maybe stepped in a little hole or something. It wasn't a big deal."

"I want you to tell me if you ever see that again," Molly said seriously. "If you ever see that again, tell me. I didn't feel anything, but you saw something, right?"

"Just for a second."

The very next day Molly had Karen X-ray the left leg and everything was fine. The ring was still there and the calcium deposits hadn't changed, and Karen did a series of mobility tests and Augie checked out just fine. For a few weeks Molly ran Augie only on the track to see if she could feel what Danny saw. Maybe they did just hit a little hole, because Augie ran as strong as ever. As was their custom, Molly threw apples to Augie and he would prance after them like a big dog. These days, she watched his every step and saw nothing wrong.

Summer vacation came once more and now was the time, according to Manny, that Molly should either train Augie to race or commit him to breeding and horse shows. Manny said two-year-old colts should run claiming races, not only to build a reputation but also to learn the game of racing. He explained that some very fast horses never won races because they started too late and were intimidated by the other horses. It is a true jockey who steers and directs his mount, but the best horses look for their own openings and never quit digging until there are no horses ahead of them. If Molly were going to learn to be a jockey, she would need to learn even more than Augie.

CHAPTER TWENTY

A Thunderous Race and a Huge Decision

Molly was deep in thought. In so many ways, she was more mother to Handsome Augie than his own mother. Her colt was the finest animal in the entire county and she made it happen. He had been a doomed foal and now he was capable of challenging any horse in the country. Dancer might be fast now, but at some point, Augie would leave him in the dust. Molly was sure that in the world of horse racing where split seconds are the margin between winning and losing, Augie might even become the next War Admiral and she stood the actual chance of being the most famous woman jockey of all time. This wasn't idle thought. These things were possible. At one time, the whole idea of Augie the runner and Molly the jockey was no more than a dream. Now, however, not only could Molly become the best known female jockey in America, but Molly actually believed Augie could beat any horse in the country.

At a group dinner Molly sat quietly and listened to conversations all around. Rosa and Manny talked about a car they wanted to buy and then Karen talked at length about her wedding dress and how she wanted to invite family members from all over the country. Dishes were passed. Molly didn't join in the conversation. Talk shifted to making Dancer an enterprise. Marty thought a fortune could be made selling shares in Dancer's future. Still Molly was silent. Manny expressed a feeling that 3-M Farm could grow into a mighty organization, especially with Karen right on the premises to take on all the veterinary business in the area, not to mention that she could care for all the existing animals with no outside fees. It was all a very grand plan, but Molly looked at her plate and picked at her food. Finally, Marty noticed his daughter.

"Hold on here a second," Marty said. "Our junior partner hasn't said a word."

"I want Augie to race the Dancer."

"What?"

"I know you heard me. I want Augie to race Dancer."

"Why?"

"Because I think Augie can beat him."

"What brings this on, little one?" Manny asked, "You don't really believe that."

"Oh, yes I do. Even you said I need to decide Augie's future and a race would help me decide."

"Molly," her father said, "this is a bad idea. First off, Dancer is a seasoned racehorse and Augie is barely two years old. He'll lose and it might set him back. You see that, don't you?"

"No, I don't see that at all."

"Did you expect Manny to ride both horses?"

"I expect to ride Augie."

"Little one," Manny said, "you don't even have the right saddle. Your father is correct. Yes, I said the handsome one is fast. He is not ready for Dancer."

"I think you're saying I'm not ready and that's the only part I might agree on with you. But don't say Augie isn't ready just because of his age. That's not fair to him."

"Can we go on to something else?" Marty asked.

"Wait a second," Karen said. "No. We can't go on to something else until we hear what Molly is saying. Why is this important to you, Molly?"

"It is important because I have worked with Augie two years of my life—every single day. No one knows Augie like

I do. Two years might not be a big deal to you, but two years is a giant part of my life. I have to know. My horse needs to know. I think it does more harm for him to zoom past Grace in every race. He'll think that's as fast as other horses can run. How fair is that to Augie and how fair is this to me?"

"I'm not saying it's forever a bad idea," her father said. "At some point, it's a good idea, but not now."

"One morning we'll wake up and it's a good idea?"

"I'm not sure I like your tone."

"I hate my tone. I don't like fighting all of you. I need to know. I just need to know."

"Enough," Marty Grimaldi announced. "When would you like this race to occur?"

"This Saturday when Danny is here."

"You want this race so your boyfriend can see it?"

"That's ridiculous and it hurts me," Molly said, sounding much older than fourteen. "I need Danny there so he can watch for something."

"What?"

"I'm not going to say. I want to race on Saturday."

"Molly," her father said, tossing his plate of half eaten food in the sink, "you have a race, young lady. Did you have a time in mind?"

"Just after sundown," Molly said defiantly. "I don't want anyone to see it from the road."

"I think you may have missed a conversation we had a few weeks back," her father said. "Manny, you have the Dancer ready. This girl will have her race. Now, if you don't mind, I have some orange groves that need my attention. Perhaps after Saturday, we'll all work together again."

Marty was angry and Karen followed him to the porch, but not in enough time to stop him from speeding away in the jeep. He bounded in the ruts and his hat flew off but he kept driving. Molly went to her room and Rosa busied herself with dishes. Manny went out to feed the cows. In her room, tears streamed down Molly's face.

Never had her father been this angry with her. Molly knew he felt betrayed and perhaps even felt she was betraying her own horse, but neither thing was true. How could she tell him? She had accomplished her goal, but at what price? The race was going to happen. That was the important thing.

The next two days were horribly uncomfortable. Her father was on a low sizzle. He was quiet and friendly, but Molly could feel the distance between them. She did her chores quickly and then took Augie out to the track to practice. First she and Augie walked three lengths of the track so her horse could understand the length of the race. Then she practiced fast starts and at the end of one length of the track she shouted, "Augie: Kick!" She meant it as an attention command and Augie didn't yet understand what it meant. She rested Augie a while, talked to him, kissed him, and then she took him back out onto the track. She saw her father watching and turned away. This time when she took Augie to a quick start and shouted, "Augie: Kick" she bore down with her heels and cracked a crop across his flank. Augie broke into a remarkable stride and stretched long legs to maximum. "Yes, baby, run!" She practiced the drill several times and each time Augie recognized the signal and seemed to zoom into another gear. She hoped he would remember. She looked toward the porch and her father was gone.

When Saturday arrived Molly was both horrified and happy her ordeal would be over. Before Danny was dropped off by his parents, Molly went to the barn for a final chat with the stallion she loved. Usually she spoke with Augie and today might be a great day for a long conversation, but she hugged him, prepared his bit and bridle, and headed back to the house. Manny stopped her along the way.

"Little one," Manny said, "I do not want this."

"Manny, we're racing horses, not one another."

"What do you want me to do?"

"I hope you're not suggesting that you should do anything but try to win. That's exactly what you should do."

"You cannot win this race."

"Not by myself. I'll bring help."

Molly and Danny stood near the barn and Danny had never seen Molly quite so quiet. He felt awkward as if he had landed in the middle of a family fight and he wasn't sure what to say.

"You sure you know what you're doing?"

"Of course not," Molly said, smiling for the first time in three days. "Listen, you're here for a reason. Take this whistle and blow it."

"What?"

"Blow it. Loud! Again! Good."

"I'm here to blow a whistle?"

"Just listen. I don't want you to do a single thing except to watch Augie's legs. You watch his legs and if he does what you saw before, you blow that whistle as loud as you can and keep blowing it."

"Why?"

"Because I'll stop. I think you saw something no one else has seen. I think that little dip you saw out in the pasture was very important. Augie's leg seems healthy, but you were the perfect person to see something was wrong."

"Wait a minute. I don't know anything about horses."

"That's the point. You saw something with new eyes and if you see it again, you blow that whistle until your eyes bug out. Do you understand me?"

"I understand, Molly. You'll wear a helmet, won't you?"

"Yes, my dad talked to me enough to say no helmet—no race. Let's go saddle Augie and you lead him out in fifteen minutes."

"I'm going to lead him out?"

"I'm not asking you to ride him. I want him skittish and nervous and you leading him out will accomplish both things. I have to change," Molly said as she walked toward the house. "Fifteen minutes and don't you forget that whistle."

Molly walked past her father and Karen and into the house. Manny and Dancer were already out on the track and Dancer looked proud and magnificent. Manny wore jeans and a regular shirt. He looked sad. There was no joy in winning a race against a colt and an inexperienced rider. He was doing as he was told, not only by Marty but Molly as well. His heart wasn't in it, except perhaps to teach a young girl and a would-be stallion an important lesson.

In her room, Molly looked at Doctor August Cable's picture and remembered how disappointed he was never to be jockey of the year. He had found other joys in life and perhaps Molly could too. She reached under her bed and pulled out the box given to her nearly two years ago. She slipped off her shirt and took Doc's silks into her hands. She looked at the label inside and she put on the shirt and buttoned the buttons at her wrists. The shirt felt sleek and silky against her skin and she buttoned down the front and looked in the mirror. She took the rubber band from her ponytail and let long hair drift across her shoulders and down her back and then she popped a half helmet on her head and snapped it under her chin. She tucked the shirt into her jeans and tried not to cry. She shoved her pant legs into her boots and took a last look in the mirror.

She paused on the porch and took in the scene at the big track. Karen recognized her father's silks and immediately buried her face in Marty's chest. Rosa stood far away from the track and watched Manny and Dancer prancing out on the track. There was Danny and Augie was trying to break away and come to her. She walked slinky-legged to the track and took Augie's reins.

"You don't have to do this," Marty said.

"Oh, yes I do. You let me warm up and then you ring the bell. Please never doubt me again."

"Molly..."

"Just ring the bell."

Molly flipped up on Augie's back, turned him through the chute, and out into the corral. She refused to look toward Manny and Dancer and took a log walk an entire length around the track. She spoke with Augie, "You remember, my baby. Only today do you run with your heart. You let it rip. You hear me?" Augie's ears were back and he picked up the pace and Molly used the opposite side of the track for a couple sprints. If Augie was ever going to be ready, he was ready now. Molly pulled even with Dancer and the older horse knew what was going to happen and Augie was not his son this day. He was another horse to be beaten. He could feel Manny's legs closing together and muscles rippled down his legs and chest. He snorted at Augie, but the colt stared straight ahead. Molly and Manny nodded toward Marty and suddenly a loud bell punctuated the stillness of the night.

Augie took off like a rocket and Molly immediately aimed him for the rail. She held the reins tight and her hair flew behind her and Doc's silks were flopping in the wind. Somehow Augie had taken the lead and held it for the first two furlongs, but soon Dancer's strides became longer and smoother and he took the lead at the first length.

Manny's backside was high in the air and the stallion thundered two lengths away and now three. Danny watched Augie's legs churning with the whistle in the corner of his mouth. Karen Cable stared at Molly and it was like watching her father race so many years ago. Dancer took the lead to four lengths and Marty turned away and looked toward the house. The second length Augie seemed to close a bit and Molly could feel him straining and stretching. "Augie: Kick!" she shouted and now her horse seemed to explode from under her and she could feel his strides fluid and coming quicker until he was a length behind at the second pole. "Augie: Kick" Molly screamed again. Marty turned around and watched his daughter take her colt to the outside and now the horses were nearly even into the backstretch. Molly went to the crop and shouted, "Run, my baby!" Augie's mane and Molly's hair mixed in the dashing wind. The finish was just ahead and Augie's neck appeared to stretch and his eyes were wild and his nostrils flared.

"Augie by a nose!" Marty shouted. "Augie by a nose. I can't believe it! Did I see this?"

Karen, Danny, and Rosa were hugging and jumping and Molly raised her fist high in the air. She pulled back Augie's reins and it took almost a furlong for him to stop. She jumped off his back and kissed Augie until she fell to the ground and now Augie licked at her face.

"I knew they couldn't beat the double-Augie! You had the legs and I had the shirt. I love you so much. Thank you, Augie. You're the best. I'll never forget this day. Aw, you have too much heart. I love you so."

A girl and her stallion walked bowlegged back toward the starting line. Karen held back the others and Marty jumped the fence and ran to his daughter.

"Molly, I was so wrong. That was the most fantastic race I have ever seen."

"It sure was something, wasn't it, Dad? I told you Augie was the best."

"It wasn't just Augie. I knew you could ride, but I had no idea. You were superb."

"Most of the time I was just hanging on. Augie runs with the wind. Wasn't it your dad who said, 'He runs like a scalded dog'? Augie was a scalded dog today, wasn't he?"

"He sure was. Do you know what this means? We have two champions now. No one would have bet that Augie could win. I'm thinking he's even faster if you had the right saddle. Can you imagine 3-M being called 'Home of the Champions'? You got what you wanted. You and Augie are on the way to great things."

"Dad," Molly said quietly, "you said Augie became my horse the moment he was born."

"Of course he is. You two will become champions and it's all your doing."

"Augie is my horse, right?"

"Yes, I said that. He is your horse. You'll get what you want."

"In that case, I never want him to race again. First Doc told me a horse runs more with his heart than his legs. Then you told me the truth of my motives would come to me one day. That day came when Danny saw a hitch in Augie's stride. I'm afraid his leg buckled for a second and I knew Augie should run with his heart at least one time. I risked that, but I don't think I want to risk him ever again. If he crumbles in the middle of a race, he's in danger and so is every other horse and rider. I won't risk Augie. He's so fast. Today I could feel that he would run right through a blowout. He can do other things."

"But what about you?"

"I won't use Augie for my benefit. I never meant to do that. I can do other things too. You and Karen, Manny and Rosa, Danny, Dancer, and my beautiful Augie—you are the things that give 3-M life and breath. I won't risk any of you."

"How old are you?" her father asked, and they walked, arm in arm, to the fence to celebrate life.